MW01180696

DAGO RED

Tales of Dark Suspense

Selected Works by Bill Pronzini

The Snatch (1971)
The Stalker (1971)
The Jade Figurine (1972)
The Vanished (1973)
Undercurrent (1973)
Snowbound (1974)
The Running of Beasts (1976)
Games (1976)
Blowback (1977)
Acts of Mercy (1977)
Twospot (1978)
Night Screams (1979)
Labyrinth (1980)
Prose Bowl (1980)
Hoodwink (1981)
Masques (1981)
The Cambodia File (1981)
Scattershot (1982)
Dragonfire (1982)
Day of the Moon (1983)
Casefile (1983)
Bindlestiff (1983)
Double (1984)
Nightshades (1984)
Quicksilver (1984)
The Eye (1984)
Bones (1985)
Quincannon (1985)
Graveyard Plots (1985)
Deadfall (1986)
Beyond the Grave (1986)
The Lighthouse (1987)
The Last Days of Horse-Shy
   Halloran (1988)
Shackles (1988)
Small Felonies (1988)

Firewind (1989)
The Hangings (1989)
Jackpot (1990)
Stacked Deck (1991)
Breakdown (1991)
Quarry (1992)
Epitaphs (1992)
Carmody's Run (1993)
Demons (1993)
The Tormentor (1994)
Hardcase (1995)
Blue Lonesome (1995)
Spadework (1996)
Sentinels (1996)
A Wasteland of Strangers (1997)
Illusions (1997)
Panic! (1997)
Carpenter and Quincannon (1998)
BoobyTrap (1998)
Nothing But the Night (1999)
Sleuths (1999)
Crazybone (2000)
Night Freight (2000)
The Gallows Land (2001)
In An Evil Time (2001)
Bleeders (2002)
Step to the Graveyard Easy (2002)
Spook (2003)
Scenarios (2003)
The Alias Man (2004)
Nightcrawlers (2005)
Quincannon's Game (2005)
Mourners (2006)
The Crimes of Jordan Wise (2006)
Savages (2007)
Fever (2008)

DAGO RED

RED

Tales of Dark Suspense

by

BILL PRONZINI

RAMBLE HOUSE

ACKNOWLEDGMENTS

"Dago Red." Copyright © 2002 by the Pronzini-Muller Family Trust. First published in *Measures of Poison.*

"I Wasn't There." Copyright © 2007 by the Pronzini-Muller Family Trust. First published in *Hollywood & Crime.*

"Me and Mitch." Copyright © 2003 by Bill Pronzini & Barry N. Malzberg. First published in *Problems Solved.*

"Possibilities." Copyright © 2005 by The Strand Magazine. First published in *The Strand Magazine.*

"Out Behind the Shed." Copyright © 1991 by the Pronzini-Muller Family Trust. First published in *Final Shadows.*

"Toiling in the Fields of the Lord." Copyright © 2008 by the Pronzini-Muller Family Trust. An original story.

"The Monster." Copyright © 1996 by the Pronzini-Muller Family Trust. First published in *Ellery Queen's Mystery Magazine.*

"Pumpkin." Copyright © 1986 by the Pronzini-Muller Family Trust. First published in *Halloween Horrors.*

"The Mayor of Asshole Valley." Copyright © 2000 by the Pronzini-Muller Family Trust. First published in *Bad News.*

"Chip." Copyright © 2001 by the Pronzini-Muller Family Trust. First published in *Mystery Scene.*

"The Winning Ticket." Copyright © 2007 by the Pronzini-Muller Family Trust. First published in *Ellery Queen's Mystery Magazine.*

"Peekaboo." Copyright © 1979 by Charles L. Grant. First published in *Nightmares.*

"Free Durt." Copyright © 2004 by the Pronzini-Muller Family Trust. First published in *Ellery Queen's Mystery Magazine.*

"Just Looking." Copyright © 2002 by the Pronzini-Muller Family Trust. First published in *Flesh & Blood: Dark Desires.*

"A Cold Foggy Day." Copyright © 1978 by the Pronzini-Muller Family Trust. First published in *Ellery Queen's Mystery Magazine.*

"The Night, the River." Copyright © 2004 by the Pronzini-Muller Family Trust. First published in *Quietly Now.*

"Cat Cay." Copyright © 1995 by the Pronzini-Muller Family Trust. First published in *Cat Crimes Takes a Vacation* as "Cat Bay on Cat Cay."

"All the Same." Copyright © 1972, 1992 by the Pronzini-Muller Family Trust. First published in *Alfred Hitchcock's Mystery Magazine.*

"Private Terrors." Copyright © 2008 by the Pronzini-Muller Family Trust. An original story.

"One Night at Dolores Park." Copyright © 1995 by the Pronzini-Muller Family Trust. First published in *Ellery Queen's Mystery Magazine.*

"Liar's Dice." Copyright © 1992 by the Pronzini-Muller Family Trust. First published in *Ellery Queen's Mystery Magazine.*

"Olaf and the Merchandisers." Copyright © 2006 by Barry N. Malzberg and Bill Pronzini. First published in *Jim Baen's Universe.*

TABLE OF CONTENTS

DAGO
RED

Tales of Dark Suspense

DAGO RED

FOG THICK as pasta sauce stirred all along the Embarcadero. Headlights crawled through it, made yellow ghost shapes out of the gray coils and threads. Out on the Bay, the foghorns sounded like women moaning in the night.

I went down the alley behind Balducci's Produce. The cobblestones were shiny-wet, empty—it was too early for Paolo to show up with the Packard touring car. There was a doorway in the building on the near side of the alley, catercorner to the one in the produce warehouse. It was deep, full of shadows. You couldn't be seen in there even on a clear night.

I'd been waiting twenty minutes when the touring car turned into the alley behind me. I drew back tight against the wall. Paolo pulled up just beyond the warehouse door, same as he always did, and left the motor running and the lights on. Little puffs of exhaust mixed with the mist. The fog churned, seemed to glow around and in front of the Packard.

The warehouse door opened and Little Jack came out. He had his hand inside his coat, but he wasn't expecting any trouble. He looked around, then made a gesture and Balducci came out. The two of them started for the touring car. I could see them plain in the glowing mist.

I stepped out and shot Little Jack first. It was a clean body shot and he went down fast. Balducci stood frozen for a second or two, his head flopping from side to side. Then he started to run back toward the warehouse door. I put a bullet in his hip just before he got there. As soon as he dropped, the Packard jumped forward and went yawing crazily down the alley into the wall of fog. That was Paolo for you. He didn't have the guts of a rabbit.

Balducci was writhing around on the cobblestones, moaning. Little Jack hadn't moved and never would again. I made sure of that before I stepped over to Balducci. I kicked him in the belly and the groin three or four times. His body jerked into a tight, cramped C and he lay there clutching himself and moaning. I could smell his breath when I leaned forward. It stank of Dago

Red. I kicked him in the face, hard, but not hard enough so he'd pass out.

I said, "Two choices, Balducci. You can take it lying down or you can get up on your feet and take it like a man."

He thought he had a third choice. His body straightened out and then he heaved up on his knees and started crying and begging, his words making little spitting bubbles through the blood on his mouth. It made me want to puke. I shot him once in the head to shut him up. Then I leaned down and shot him twice more, left eye, right eye, to make sure.

It was dark in the apartment. Through the big bay window I could make out a couple of streetlamps like eyes in the fog. On a clear night you'd be able to see the lights on Alcatraz out in the Bay. It was a fancy apartment, high up on Russian Hill—thick carpets, expensive furniture. It must've cost Balducci two hundred a month, easy.

A key scraped in the lock and the front door opened. Gina stood there, backlit by the wall sconces in the hallway. "Al? Why've you got the lights off?"

I sat quiet, waiting.

She walked on in, shut the door behind her. "Al?" Then the ceiling globe came on.

I said, "Al's not home."

"Joey!"

"He's not coming home. Not tonight, not ever."

"Oh my God!" Her face was white as milk, her eyes wide, scared.

"You shouldn't've done it, Gina."

"It's not what you think, I—"

"It's just what I think. I know all about it. So does Renzo."

"Joey . . . please, you have to listen—"

"Why should I?"

She took a step toward me. Expensive perfume and expensive liquor came off her in waves. She was wearing the sable coat Renzo had given her. She'd dyed her hair a lighter blonde and had it marceled—the light from the ceiling globe made it look varnished. She looked expensive and cheap at the same time, like one of the women in Fat Leona's high-class bawdy house.

"Joey, please . . . I couldn't help it, it wasn't my fault. I had to do something, I was going crazy. Renzo . . . you think he's a swell guy but he's not. You don't know how mean he can be. He knocks me around, he—"

I said, "You shouldn't have done it," and got up on my feet.

She saw the gun for the first time and said, "Oh God, no, you can't, you wouldn't!" in a low moany voice. "Not you, not you!"

"You shouldn't've done it, Gina."

She sucked in air and her red mouth opened wide.

I stopped her before she could start screaming. One clean shot was all it took.

The fog was even thicker down by Islais Creek. I had to grope my way around to the back of the Bay Area Distributors warehouse. The third time I knocked on the door, the peephole slid back and Mac looked out. He said, "Hey, Joey, you're late. Where you been?" He didn't know about Balducci and Gina. Nobody knew except Renzo and me.

"Things to do," I said. "Hurry up, it's cold out here."

The locks rattled and he let me in. He had a Thompson gun in the crook of his left arm. Guido and Tony and a bunch of others were grouped around the big canvas-sided trucks, a Graham and two new Macks they'd brought over from Friendly's Garage. Some of them had choppers, too. A ship was down from Canada, anchored beyond the three-mile limit off the Sonoma County coast, and we had a two A.M. meet with the fishing boats that ran the whiskey in to one of the beaches south of Bodega Bay. We'd haul the cases back here in the trucks, get them ready for distribution. The fix was in with the county sheriff and the city coppers. We never had any trouble with them. You always had to worry about the Feds, but Balducci's crowd was the reason for all the extra heat.

I said to Mac, "Where's Renzo?"

"Waiting upstairs."

The stairs were at the far wall, the only break in the stacks of wine barrels, sacks of sugar, crates of jackass brandy and bonded Canadian hooch. You could smell the wine in there. It was good, pre-Prohibition Burgundy from the counties up north, but it still smelled sour to me—no better than Dago Red. You couldn't smell it from outside. The walls were thick concrete with wood facing. The place was like a fortress.

Renzo was behind the desk in his office. He had a glass of whiskey in one hand, a Toscanelli stogie in the other. He didn't look good. His long face was white, sweaty, and his eyes had a funny glass shine when he looked up at me. Like a dead man's eyes.

I said, "It's done."

"Both of them?"

"Both of them."

Renzo said, "Christ," and sucked hard on his Toscanelli. He was always smoking those stinking tule roots. I couldn't stand them myself. You had to drag hard just to get smoke from one end to the other and you couldn't get enough to inhale.

I said, "What time do we move out tonight?"

"Midnight. You don't need to go along."

"I don't mind. I'll ride shotgun with Guido in the Graham."

He gave me a long look. Then he got up and wandered around and stopped at the back wall, stood staring at the calendar hanging there. It was a San Francisco Chamber of Commerce calendar, with a picture of Cliff House and February 1930 showing.

He said, "How bad was it?" softly.

"Gina? Not as bad as I thought it'd be."

"You did it quick? She didn't suffer?"

"No."

"Balducci?"

"Not so quick. He took it on his knees, begging."

"Yeah? Begging? Good."

"Little Jack's dead too."

Renzo said, "That don't break my heart," and came back to his desk sucking on that tule root. He still looked sick. He tossed off what was left in his glass, poured it half full again. "Pour yourself one, Joey."

I got a glass, splashed in two fingers, tasted it. Canadian Club. Nothing but the best for Renzo. I took the glass over to where the calender hung, tore off the February page. Today's date was Thursday, March 5. He never did pay any attention to little things like that.

"Christ, I wish it hadn't had to be like this," he said. "I loved her. You know that, Joey."

"Sure, I know it."

"A lush, a *scopona*. A traitor. Doublecrossing me with Balducci, that was bad enough. But those hijacks down the Peninsula, up north . . . how'd Balducci know where to jump the trucks if he didn't get it from Gina? Nobody else knew, just you and me—not even Guido and Mac, the last time. It had to be Gina. In bed, bed talk. He screws her, then he screws us."

"Not any more."

"No, by Christ, not any more. *Noi sono levato Balducci nostro coglioni, eh?*"

"Si. Per sempre."

Renzo swallowed more Canadian Club, fast, as if it was water. "She was like a bad barrel of wine," he said. Soft again, almost like he was talking to himself. "Fine Burgundy, young, sweet, then all of a sudden she went bad. Like maybe a bung worked loose in her head, too much air got in."

He'd said all of this before, last night. But if he wanted to say it again, that was all right with me.

"We had to do it," he said. "She might've gone to the Feds when she heard about Balducci. We had to do it, Joey."

"That's right. We didn't have any choice."

"I wish it could've been somebody besides you, but who else could I trust to do it right, Balducci and her both?"

"There wasn't anybody else," I said. "Just me."

The old lady was in the kitchen, drinking wine and reading the Bible, when I came into the house in North Beach. She'd been crying. Wet glistened like little rivers in the seams and lines of her face.

"You hear, Guiseppe? You know about poor Gina?"

"I heard."

"Atroce! Somebody kill her, shoot her like a dog. Why, why?"

"Maybe she doublecrossed somebody."

"Bah!" She made the sign of the cross. "Poor Gina, she's a nice girl, she never hurt nobody."

"She hurt plenty of people," I said.

"I don't believe it, not my Gina. What'sa matter with you? No tears, no sadness in your face. You don't care she's gone, she's killed? Your little sister?"

"She was no good, Mama."

The old bitch gave me the evil eye. She said, *"Silenzio! Tu parla quando pisciano legalline!"* and reached for the wine bottle. Dago Red. All she ever drinks is that goddamn Dago Red.

I WASN'T THERE

THEY HAD the car ready when the cab dropped us off at Brady's Garage in West L.A. It was a Packard touring car, shiny black, the side curtains already buttoned up. Nick walked around it a couple of times, kicked the tires, stuck his head inside.

"New, huh?" he said to Brady.

"Nineteen thirty model, only been available a couple of months. Fit right in where you're going."

"Yeah?"

"Yeah. It's the older models stand out up there."

"Take your word for it," I said. "What about this finger man?"

"Fenner."

"Yeah, Fenner. Dependable?"

"Hundred percent," Brady said. "Been hanging on Macklin's coattails ever since he spotted him."

"So there won't be no slipups tonight?"

"None. Count on it."

"Okay. Take your word on that too."

"You boys know how to get to the Hollywood Plaza? I got some maps in my office . . ."

Nick said, "You think we ain't looked at maps already?"

"Just making sure."

"We're the best Renzo's got. He must've told you."

"Sure, he told me."

"We don't make mistakes. We don't overlook nothing."

"That's what he said. I wish I had a couple like you in my outfit."

"You ain't the first to say it, Mr. Brady."

"Come on," I said to Nick, "we're wasting time. Let's get rolling."

Nick liked driving the new Packard. He kept grinning and smacking the wheel with his hand. He was crazy about cars. He'd rather have a car to play with than a woman. There wasn't a better wheel man on a job like this. Or for a fast getaway when you needed one, like the time the Feds ambushed us while we were

helping offload a shipment of Canadian whiskey up by Bodega
Bay. Hadn't been for Nick that night, we'd've both been in a fed-
eral pen now.

It didn't take us too long to get to Hollywood. "Hey," Nick
said, "hey, Joey. Hollywood Boulevard, huh?"

"Yeah."

"Look at the people, everybody dressed up fit to kill. And the
cars, nothing but the best. Rolls, Bugattis, Duesies—that Duesen-
berg J over there, that's the third one I seen already. Yeah, and all
the neon. One A.M. and everything's lit up like New Year's Eve."

"Too many lights."

"Won't make no difference. Remember what Brady said? Everybody minds his own business down here, no matter what time it
is."

"Yeah."

"It'll go easy, no sweat."

"You ever see me sweat? No, and you never will."

"Man, I can't get over the traffic this time of night. And so
many of the flash crowd out partying. Bet most of 'em are in the
moving picture racket."

"Couldn't prove it by me."

"Maybe we'll recognize somebody."

"Yeah. Macklin."

"No, I mean somebody famous. Actors, actresses. Chaplin and
Buster Keaton, them two I'd like to meet. Find out if they're as
funny in person, you know? They make me laugh every time I see
'em on the screen." He laughed to prove it and smacked the steering wheel again. "Norma Shearer, Joan Crawford, Greta Garbo.
Yeah, Garbo. And Mary Pickford and that gee she's married to,
Fairbanks."

"I wouldn't know any of 'em if they jumped on the running
board."

"Don't you never go to the pictures, Joey?"

"No."

"You must've been sometime."

"Once or twice, years ago. Make-believe don't interest me."

"What does, besides the skirts?"

"Speaks. Hot jazz."

"Yeah, sure," Nick said. "But I like the pictures too. The silents,
they were good, that Chaplin kills me, but the talkies, they're even
better. You don't have to read them subtitles. And the actresses,

they all got voices like they're whispering in your ear in bed, you know what I mean?"

"I never heard an actress whisper."

"I wonder what they'd be like in bed. Garbo, Crawford, Thelma Todd, swell dames like that."

"Like any other dame with her clothes off."

"Nah, better. Tits, gams, asses—all better or they wouldn't be actresses. Give you the ride of your life, huh?"

"You'll never know," I said.

He laughed and smacked the wheel. "Hey, there's Musso and Franks Grill. Plenty of movie stars hang out there. Too bad we ain't got time to go in, look around. Bet they got some real good liquor in their speak."

We been working together three years now, me and Nick. If I got any friend in Renzo's outfit it's Nick Coletti. He's a good boy, but that's the trouble, he's a twenty-five year old boy don't seem able to grow up all the way. Gets himself excited about things that don't matter. Cars, horse races, poker, baseball. And now this Hollywood crap. Like he was some goddamn hayseed from Iowa. He grates on my nerves sometimes.

"Kid in a candy store," I said.

"Huh?"

"How much farther to the hotel?"

"Vine Street's just up ahead. Plaza's around the corner."

"Don't park right in front. Or under a street light."

"You think I don't know better than that?"

"Yeah. Okay."

"There's the Melody Club," he said. "Brady's finger man . . . what's his name again?"

"Fenner."

"He better be inside that joint with Macklin."

"Getting him primed. Macklin likes his hooch."

"Better not let him leave too early."

"He won't. Brady wouldn't steer us wrong about Fenner. Him and Renzo go way back."

"That Macklin," Nick said. "Pretty stupid bird, huh?"

"He thought he could get away with it."

"They always think that. But nobody ever does."

"That's right," I said. "Nobody ever does."

We turned the corner onto Vine Street and Nick found a place to park. "Hey, Joey, Hollywood and Vine, huh?" he said and started rattling off more names that didn't mean nothing to me.

Sardi's Diner, Brown Derby, Hollywood Playhouse, some fancy
theater they were putting up on the corner, some building where
Chaplin had his offices. The only place I cared about was the
Plaza Hotel. It was right down the block, big neon sign all lit up on
the roof, doorman, three or four cabs lined up in front. But we
were far enough away and it was dark enough here. Just some
nightlights behind a store window across the sidewalk.

"The It Cafe," Nick said.

"The what?"

"It Cafe. In the Plaza Hotel."

"What the hell kind of name is that, the It Cafe?"

"Clara Bow owns it. You know, the It Girl."

"Another actress."

"No, she's something special. They named her right. That
dame's got it and then some."

"Yeah? Somebody give her a shot of penicillin, then she won't
have it no more."

He laughed hard enough to cough and thumped the steering
wheel. "That's good, Joey. That's rich. 'Somebody give her a shot
of penicillin, she won't have it no more.' I got to remember that."

"What time is it?"

"Must be close to midnight."

"Check and make sure."

He opened his pocket watch, held it up close and squinted at it.
"Eleven fifty. Won't be long now."

It wasn't too long. Less than twenty minutes. I spotted them
first, crossing the street at the corner. Macklin and a tubby little
guy with an arm around his shoulder, steering him. They came
down the sidewalk on the side we were on. Macklin looked pretty
steady on his feet. He always could hold his liquor.

"Here they come," Nick said.

I got my rod out, slid it into my coat pocket. They were about
ten paces from the car when I opened the door and stepped out.
Brady's finger man, Fenner, did a fast fade as soon as he saw me.
Macklin didn't know what was happening until I stepped in close
and jabbed the gun into his belly.

"Stand still, Mac."

"Joey!" He knew then and his eyes bugged. Their eyes always
bug when they see you and feel the rod. They know right away
their number's up. "Oh Jesus, no."

"Get in the car."

"Listen, listen . . ."

"In the car or you get it right here."

He sagged a little and I had to hold him up, prod him over to the Packard. Nick had the motor running. A couple went by on the sidewalk, the woman draped in furs, but they didn't pay no attention to us. I opened the door, shoved Macklin inside, crowded in after him.

Nick said, "Hiya, Mac."

"Oh Jesus," Macklin said.

Nick got us rolling. Macklin slid over against the far door. I could see the whites of his bugged eyes in the darkness.

"What's the idea?" he said. "Joey, Nick?"

"Don't play dumb," I said. "It won't do you no good."

"Renzo sent you? All the way from Frisco? Why?"

"San Francisco," Nick said. "You lived there long enough, you know we don't like it called Frisco."

"What'd I do? What's Renzo think I done?"

"Tell him, Nick."

"Oakland warehouse raid," Nick said. "Six weeks ago."

"What's that got to do with me?"

"Somebody tipped the Feds about the load of jackass brandy coming in. You, Mac."

"No! It wasn't me." He was sweating now. You could smell the liquor he'd been drinking, the fear that came oozing out with the sweat. "Why would I tip the Feds?"

"Forty grand, that's why."

"The payoff money? The Feds got it along with the shipment."

"They didn't get it."

"They must've. How you know they didn't?"

"The same way we know you tipped 'em," I said. "Renzo's got a pipeline. Not direct, so it took a while, but the word come through. You didn't figure on that, did you?"

"I tell you, I didn't take that dough. You think I'm crazy?"

"You and Garza were the bag men that night."

"Then Garza must've took it. It wasn't me."

"Garza didn't take it."

"How you know he didn't?"

"He stayed home," Nick said. "You hung around a while and then quit and come down here."

"I didn't quit," Macklin said. "I fell into a better deal. I told Renzo and he said it was okay."

"It ain't okay anymore."

"Yeah, a better deal," I said. "Some boys from Encino."

"That's right."

"That's wrong. Nobody in Encino ever heard of Frank Macklin."

"You talked to the wrong people. This is a new outfit, they got a deal worked out with some Mexican shippers. I'll give you their names . . ."

"Buy a lot of lies with forty grand."

"I tell you, I didn't take that dough. It must've been Garza."

"It wasn't Garza," Nick said. "Garza lived in a roach trap in the Tenderloin, same like always. Didn't change nothing in his life. You live high on the hog in the Hollywood Plaza Hotel."

"What you mean, he *lived* in a roach trap? He's not there anymore? He must've took a run-out powder. You found me, can't you find him?"

"Sure we can. We know right where he is."

"Whyn't you go after him then? Take him for a ride?"

"We can't do that."

"Why can't you?"

"He's down in Colma, six feet under."

"Dead? Garza's dead?"

"Hit and run on the Embarcadero, right around the time you blew town."

"You think I done that too? I didn't!"

"Might've been an accident," Nick said. "Or somebody with a grudge. I figure it was a gee named Macklin trying to protect his ass."

"It wasn't me. How many times I have to say it!"

"Let's have your wallet, Mac," I said.

He didn't move. I reached over with my left hand, opened his overcoat, yanked the wallet out of his pocket. Fat. You could choke a cat with the wad of greenbacks in there.

"How much you got here? Couple of grand?"

"The boys from Encino, they pay big. Thousand a week."

"Sure they do," Nick said.

"I'll cut you in. Five, maybe ten grand apiece. How's that sound?"

"Sounds like what's left of Renzo's forty."

"No, no—"

"Might as well tell us where you got it stashed. We'll find it anyway."

"All the dough I got's in my room at the Plaza. Maybe fifteen grand. But it's Encino money, I swear it. Those boys out there—"

"Yeah, we know. They pay big."

"That's right. Big."

"Not as big as tipping the Feds when you're a bag man for forty grand."

"I didn't take it, I didn't!"

"Nobody else at the warehouse that night," Nick said. "Except Garza and he's out. That leaves you."

"Wait a minute," Macklin said. "Wait a minute now."

"We're all through waiting."

"No, wait a minute. Listen. Garza and me, we weren't the only ones there that night. Somebody else was there too."

"Yeah? Who?"

"Joey. *Joey* was there."

"Bullshit," Nick said.

"No, it's true. I just remembered. I remember now."

"I wasn't there," I said.

"Nick, listen, Joey was there. He showed up right after Garza and me got to the warehouse. Right before the Feds broke in."

"Bullshit."

"I wasn't anywhere near Oakland that night," I said.

"He come in, I saw him, and then all hell bust loose and me and Garza powdered. The satchel was on the desk in the office. Joey must've took it."

"Bullshit," Nick said.

"Joey, you son of a bitch, *you* took that money, not me!"

I slapped him across the mouth, hard. "Shut up, Mac."

"You're the one run over Garza, too. Sure, sure, shut him up so he couldn't tell you was there—"

I clubbed him with the gun this time. The sight opened up a gash on his cheek that spurted blood. He yelled and cringed back and his head smacked into the side curtain, made it jiggle.

"You say another word, I'll give it to you right here. In the belly, where it hurts the most."

He started to moan.

"Cut it out," Nick said, "for Chrissake."

Macklin didn't cut it out. He just cowered over there against the door like a kicked dog, whimpering.

We were climbing into the hills now, up behind Hollywood. Narrow twisty roads, hardly any traffic. Down below there were plenty of lights, big dazzle spread out wide, but it seemed pretty dark up here.

Nick said, "Man, look at that view. This Hollywood's really something, hey?"

"Find a spot," I said.

Macklin moaned and whimpered. He kept saying, "Oh Jesus," over and over, like he was praying. In the glow from the dashboard, blood gleamed black on his cheek and hand. Brady wasn't going to like it when we brought the Packard back with blood on the seat.

The hell with Brady.

"Dirt road up ahead," Nick said.

"Houses?"

"No houses. Just trees."

"Pull off there."

The Packard bounced and slid a little as he turned off the pavement. Once we were in among the trees, you couldn't see the light dazzle any more. Real dark except for the headlamps.

"Looks good right here."

"Leave the headlights on," I said.

"You think I don't know that, Joey?"

Macklin was holding his face in both hands now. "Oh Jesus," he said between his fingers.

The tires crunched over something and we stopped. Nick set the brake, left the engine running and the lights on.

"All right," I said to Macklin. "Get out."

"No. No! Nick, you got to listen to me—"

"Shut up. Get out."

"No. Please . . ."

Nick got out and opened the back door. Macklin almost fell out. Nick pulled him the rest of the way, shoved him up against the side of the car. I slid out alongside. It was dark as hell up here, woods closed in tight against the road. If it weren't for the headlamps, you couldn't't've seen ten feet in front of you.

Macklin started to slide down the side of the Packard, like he didn't have bones in his legs anymore. Nick hauled him up again. "Come on, Macklin," he said. "Stand up and take it like a man."

"You got to believe me—it was Joey, *it was Joey!*"

"I'm sick of listening to him," I said. "Let's get it done."

Nick backed off a few steps. He already had his rod out.

All of a sudden Macklin yelled and shoved off the car and tried to run into the trees. He ran like a woman, all floppy arms and legs, yelling the whole time.

He didn't get ten yards before I shot him. Three times, fast. All the slugs went in under his shoulder blades. I never miss at that range—I wouldn't've missed even if he hadn't been running right through the headlight beams. He flopped down on his face and lay there with one leg twitching. Nick went over and put two more into him to make sure.

I frisked him for his hotel room key and we got back into the Packard. Neither of us said anything until we were out on the paved road again. Then I said, "I wasn't there that night, Nick."

"Sure, I know," he said.

"Macklin was just trying to buy time, drive a wedge between us."

"I never believed him for a minute."

But he was wondering just the same. I could hear it in his voice.

Next afternoon we rode a cab to Union Station and caught the Coast Flyer for San Francisco. Nick had been real quiet all day—no more Hollywood talk, not much talk about anything. Couple of times I caught him looking at me with a funny look on his pan. And he wanted to hold the fifteen grand cash we took out of Macklin's room at the Plaza, be the one to hand it over to Renzo. "You know, Joey, just to have the feel of that much dough for a while."

He was wondering, all right.

On the trip down we'd had meals together, played euchre in the smoker. Not this trip. He went to his compartment right after we got on board. Said he wasn't feeling so hot and didn't want dinner.

You could see what would happen once we got to San Francisco. He'd do more than deliver the fifteen grand, he'd tell Renzo what Macklin said about me being at the warehouse that night. Probably Renzo wouldn't believe it. But maybe he would. I couldn't take the chance.

Sometime during the night I'd have to bump Nick off.

Make it look like an accident. Catch him off guard, sap him, toss him off the train. People get drunk on bootleg hooch, fall off trains all the time. Nobody'd figure it for anything else. Renzo wouldn't.

It was a dirty shame. I liked Nick, he'd saved my bacon that time up at Bodega Bay, he was the only friend I had. But what else could I do? I *wasn't* at the warehouse that night. I didn't tip off the Feds, I didn't take the payoff money, I didn't run over Garza on the Embarcadero, I didn't have nothing to do with any of it. But that bastard Macklin had planted a seed in Nick's head, and if I let Nick plant it in Renzo's, then maybe it'd be me got picked up next for a one-way ride. I just couldn't risk it.

You got to look out for yourself in this business. Yeah, you do. Ain't nobody else gonna do it for you.

ME AND MITCH

(with Barry N. Malzberg)

WELL, ALL THIS HAPPENED a long time ago. Almost fifty years. Dodgers were still in Brooklyn where they belonged and Ebbets Field was still the best place in the country to watch a ball game, never mind what the Cubs fans say about Wrigley. Draft beer was two bits a schooner, you could eat a big meal for a buck at Longchamps, the Rockettes were still kicking at Radio City Music Hall, and if you took a date to Coney Island you still had a chance to get lucky under the boardwalk.

Better world back then. Some people say so, anyway. Me, I don't think so. World was just as crazy in those days, what with the polio scare and Korea and everybody worried that the Russians would drop the bomb. People were just as crazy, too—hurting each other, hurting themselves.

Me and Mitch and a bunch of other regulars used to hang out at Mooney's Saloon, an old workingman's tavern in the shadow of Ebbets. Two generations of Mooneys had kept it operating for better than sixty years, even during Prohibition; old man Mooney said nobody but God Almighty could tell him not to serve cold beer to a thirsty man, and he paid graft to pretty much run wide open for the duration. Place had a brass rail, spittoons, sawdust on the floor, big crock of pickled eggs on the bar. And framed, signed photos of sports greats on the walls. Fighters like Dempsey and Louis and Marciano, but mainly Bums. Durocher, Jackie Robinson, Pee Wee Reese, the Duke, the Preacher, dozens more. Not Ralph Branca, though, not after he served up that fat home run curve to Bobby Thompson in '51. Night that happened, Mitch tore Branca's photo off the wall and stomped it into the floor and nobody tried to stop him.

We were both from the neighborhood, me and Mitch. Both young punks, both worked construction, both liked to shoot pool and sip suds and play the pinball machines. Bar buddies, not real friends. Didn't see much of each other outside of Mooney's, except once in a while we'd take in a game at Ebbets or roll a few lines for brews at Studemeyer's Bowlarama. Different guys away from the tavern, you know what I mean? Different as night and day.

Thing about Mitch, he was a little guy wanted to be a big guy. Wore his hair in a slicked-back ducktail like Elvis, wore T-shirts with a pack of Camels rolled up in one sleeve. Talked tough and swaggered when he had a load on. Nobody paid much attention to him; even Swede Johannsen, who seemed to be a genuine tough guy, pretty much ignored Mitch when he started mouthing off. So did I. He was all bark and no bite. That's what everybody thought, anyhow.

Back then, I went by Lenny. Actually my name's Leonard, which is what I preferred to be called when I was away from Mooney's. Now that the L.A. Dodgers are a joke and about bankrupt thanks to the sellout to that bastard Murdoch, now that the world's gone crazy again, I prefer L. J. Don't ask me why. It's just what I prefer, that's all, even though Gloria, my late wife, was of the opinion that it's kind of sad when a guy my age changes his name for no good reason. Yeah, I know this has nothing much to do with what happened; it's just background information of the kind that Branch Rickey wanted on Jackie Robinson before he signed him to that first contract. Or, hell, maybe it does have something to do with it. I don't know.

Delaying the story is what I'm doing, I guess, the way I was delaying real life back there in Mooney's nearly fifty years ago. The way you do when you're young and single and don't have a mortgage and money troubles and all the rest of it. You know what I mean?

I'd've gone on delaying my life and me and Mitch would've gone on being bar buddies for who knows how long, even after O'Malley yanked the Dodgers out of Brooklyn and hauled them all the way out to La La Land, if it hadn't been for Stella Kleinfelt. Swede Johannsen, too, but mainly Stella. After what happened with them, nothing was ever the same again. Not for any of us.

This Stella was Patsy Dorfman's cousin, from over in Jersey. She'd got a job in the city and moved in with Patsy until she could find a place of her own, and they'd just started coming into Mooney's. She was sure something to look at, Stella was. Big woman—not fat, just big all over, close to six feet tall with blond hair and Monroe-type boobs in a push-up bra. All the guys had a letch for her, but the ones that drooled the most were Mitch and Swede Johannsen.

The Swede was big, too. And he liked to hear himself talk, the same as Mitch. Always yacking about his life, his tryout with the Senators in '48 and how they offered him a Class D contract which he was too proud to take, and his deal with Rheingold for an exclusive distributorship and the crew he had doing all the work while he raked in the lion's share, and what a big stud he was. We pretty much figured most of it was bullshit, but who could tell with a guy like that? He looked tough and acted tough and claimed he carried a gun because one of his delivery slaves had threatened him and he wasn't taking any chances. So nobody called him a liar. Nobody messed with him, either.

He was there that night, carrying a bigger load than usual on account of some deal he was bragging on. Me and Mitch were playing pinball. Mitch had a load on, too, and when Stella and Patsy walked in he stopped and stared and licked his chops. She looked oh so fine in a tight red dress, those headlights bulging half out of the top.

"Man," he said in that cocky way of his. "Man oh man oh man."

"Forget it, Mitch," I said.

"Forget what?"

"You'll never get next to her. None of us will."

"You wanna bet? I seen the way she looks at me sometimes."

"That's all in your head. She's not interested in anybody, she comes in for the same reason we do—to have a good time."

"I got a good time I can give her."

"Yeah, sure. Lookit—Swede's already moving in on her."

"Hell with that big jerk." He pasted a Camel to his lower lip, left it there unlit. But he didn't do anything else. Just stood there holding his bottle of Rheingold and sucking on his unlit Camel and staring at Stella.

The Swede was moving in on her, all right. He'd done it before, just as fast, and every time she'd held him off at arm's length like she did every other guy in Mooney's. Only this night he didn't back off. He started whispering to her real earnest, like he was telling her all the secrets of the universe. All she did was laugh and pay more attention to Patsy than she did to him. Then he started pawing her a little, slobbering on her neck. She didn't like that. She told him to cut it out. He was the one who laughed then, loud, like a donkey braying.

Mitch started to get steamed, watching. His hand got tight around the neck of the Rheingold bottle like maybe he was imag-

ining it was the Swede's neck. "The big slob," he said. "If he don't
leave her alone . . ."

"What do you care? It's none of your business."

"She deserves to be treated better than that. I ought to go over
there and tell him off."

"You don't want to do that. Stay out of it." That was Brooklyn
wisdom then and probably now. You stayed out of trouble whenever you could, especially bar fights. Things had to jump all over
you first, and even then you fought only to save your own ass, not
some other guy's.

The Swede whispered something else to Stella. This time she
glared at him. So he laughed loud and swigged his brew and then
nibbled her ear again. Whatever it was he said that time, she
turned bright red, jerked around on her stool, and belted him
across the face.

She was a big woman and she put a lot of muscle into that
roundhouse slap. It knocked Swede right off his stool, spilled beer
all over the front of his pants. The regulars couldn't help but bust
out laughing. The laughter as much as the slap yanked the Swede's
chain. He sat there for about five seconds, fuming, and then he
hauled off and whacked her as hard as she'd whacked him.

Well, that was too much for Mitch. The rest of us just stood
around gawking, while Stella started bawling and rubbing her
cheek, but Mitch took off running across the sawdust to the bar.
He stopped in front of the Swede and leaned up in his face and
said, "What's the idea hitting a woman, you big son of a bitch?"

It got real quiet in there. If there'd been a ballgame on that
night, you'd've been able to hear the crack of a bat over at Ebbets.

The Swede loomed over him by a good eight inches, but Mitch
had more guts than we'd given him credit for. He stood his
ground.

"Who you calling a son of a bitch?"

"You, you son of a bitch."

"Say that again and I'll bust your head for you."

Mitch had just enough of a load on, and just enough of a letch
for Stella, to say it again. And sure enough, the Swede busted his
head. I mean that's just what he did. He hit Mitch three times in
the face, right, left, right, so fast that his hands were a blur. Mitch
went down and sailed backward through the sawdust until he
smacked up against the pool table. His head was all bloody and his
eyes were glazed over. He didn't move. Down for the count.

I started over to help him, but the Swede got there first. He was half crazy by then and he picked Mitch up and started beating on him some more. Must've punched him half a dozen times before me and some of the other regulars pulled him off.

Mitch was in a bad way. The bartender, Herman, called for medical help but he didn't call the law. In Brooklyn back then you didn't have anything to do with the law if you could avoid it. Swede left before the ambulance guys got there, muttering and grumbling and glaring; nobody tried to stop him.

Well, Mitch ended up in the hospital with a broken nose, busted cheekbone, three teeth knocked out, and assorted cuts and abrasions. Some of us went to see him. He claimed Stella came to see him, too, told him how sorry she was and what a brave thing he'd done for her and held his hand for him, but we didn't believe it. He had a lot of fantasies, Mitch did, where women were concerned.

He could've pressed assault charges against the Swede, but he didn't. I asked him why and he said, "I'll fix that bastard my own way one of these days. I'll fix him good."

"You don't mean you're gonna go gunning for him?"

"You'll find out, Lenny. When the time comes."

The Swede quit coming into Mooney's. So did Stella and Patsy. And Mitch didn't show when he got out of the hospital. I was still hanging out there some evenings, because I wasn't ready to move on yet and didn't have anywhere else to go. That's where I was about a week later, when we heard what'd happened on the TV news.

The Swede had been found in an alley next to Patsy Dorfman's apartment house, shot to death with his own gun.

I guess it was natural enough that Mitch would be suspected of being the shooter, after the fight in Mooney's. Everybody sure figured he was guilty when he all of a sudden disappeared, two days after Swede was found. Cops came around to the tavern to talk to us regulars, and one of them let it slip that they'd grilled Mitch and when they went around to his place to grill him again, he was gone bag and baggage.

Well, you'd think the law would've made an effort to find him. But I doubt that they did. No cops ever came around to Mooney's again, or talked to any of us individually that I know about, and I figure that after a week or so they back-burnered the whole thing. Fact was, Swede Johannsen wasn't an important or even a respectable citizen. Turned out his Rheingold distributorship was just a lot of hooey—he'd been nothing more than a deliveryman himself—and he had a shady past to boot. Convicted once of assault and once of possession of an illegal firearm. Plus he had no flock of friends or family demanding justice. Neither did Mitch, for that matter. These were just casual guys in casual times, if you catch my drift.

None of the bar regulars cared much, either. The Swede had been nobody's pal and Mitch had been only what you call an on-premises friend to me and most of the others. I hoped he'd stay lost—I wished him well, but I didn't miss him even a little. As I'd said to him once, "Mitch, I don't think I've ever seen you without half a bag on." We'd laughed at that, but looking back I can see it wasn't funny. A hell of a comment on the way we lived in those days, you know? Lenny the Loser hanging out with Mitch the Loser and Swede the Loser and all the other Losers in the shadow of Ebbets Field.

Stella, though—Stella was a different story.

The day Mitch disappeared, I went over to see her at Patsy Dorfman's and she wasn't there. Patsy said she'd decided all of a sudden to quit her job and go back to Jersey. Maybe Patsy believed that and maybe she was covering up, I don't know. All I know is that I contacted Stella's folks and some of her friends over in Jersey, and if any of them knew where she was they wouldn't tell me.

Once the news that Stella had also disappeared got circulated in Mooney's, there was all sorts of speculation.

One theory was that she was dead, that Mitch had killed her, too, for some crazy reason, and chucked her body in the East River. The other theory was that the two of them had been secret lovers and had run off together, which made a lot more sense. That was pretty much the way I saw it. Remember what Mitch had said about her coming to see him in the hospital and holding his hand? It hadn't been a fantasy after all.

The talk went on for a while and then, with nothing to feed it, it died out. Before long nobody even mentioned Mitch or Stella or the Swede anymore. Life moves on. O'Malley was cooking his plan to split Flatbush with the Dodgers, teasing the mayor, Robert Wagner, with the possibility that he'd stay and poor Wagner, a hard-of-hearing bum, didn't realize that the fix was already made. Then O'Malley pulled Horace Stoneham on board and made his announcement that the Giants were heading west, too. That was all anybody in Mooney's talked about or cared about from then until I finally quit hanging out there and got on with my life.

Is that all to the story? No. Hell, no. You been patient, sitting there listening to me talk and wondering if I'd ever get to the point, and don't think I don't appreciate it. So I'll buy you another drink before closing time and tell you the rest of it. It's time I told it, straight out. Maybe it will do me some good to get it told. But I doubt it. Nothing about what happened back there in Brooklyn ever did me any good.

Mitch didn't shoot the Swede in that alley next to Patsy Dorfman's building. I guess you could say I shot him, but the real truth is, he shot himself.

No, it wasn't suicide. What happened was this: That night, late, I was half in the bag when I left Mooney's, feeling lonesome and wanting company, so I went over to see Stella. She wasn't there, but the Swede was. Waiting for her outside, even drunker than I was and in one of his mean moods. He started throwing his weight around, bragging on how he planned to put that little bastard Mitch back into the hospital for a lot longer stay next time he saw him. It rubbed me the wrong way, and I called him on it. He said, nasty, "You in love with Mitch, maybe? Maybe I oughta put you in the hospital too, both of you in the same bed."

I didn't bite on that, but then he started in on Stella. What a sweet piece she was, how he couldn't wait to get next to her, what he would do to her when he did. That was what put me over the line, that and all the Rheingold I'd thrown down my neck. I jumped him and while we were wrestling in that alley, he yanked his gun out and tried to brain me with it. I got hold of his wrist, and the next thing I knew the gun went off and the Swede grunted and quit fighting and then quit moving. Bullet went straight through his heart. Alive one second, dead the next.

Well, I got away fast without being seen, and nobody ever knew I was there. I never told anyone until tonight. Maybe I'd've told Mitch if he hadn't disappeared, but probably not. I don't think he ever suspected me. Or that Stella did, either.

What happened to the two of them? I never found out. Only thing I know for sure is that they ran off together. Stella and Mitch, an unlikely couple, but the world is full of unlikely couples. I like to believe that wherever they went they've been happy. Had and are still having a beautiful life together.

I guess you've figured out by now why I feel that way. Sure, that's right. I was in love with Stella myself. I'd've been good to her, too, maybe just as good as Mitch if I'd had the chance. But I didn't. I never had any luck at all.

Sometimes—lately, a lot of the time—I think what my life might've been like if Stella hadn't fallen in love with Mitch, if the Swede hadn't blown himself up and in a way blown me up along with him. If I'd stayed in Brooklyn, instead of moving out here to Southern California—running out on my roots the same as the Dodgers did in '57. I'm pretty sure it would've been better than the life I've had. More real. More honest.

But here I am, an old man now, a widower alone after thirty years of a loveless, childless marriage, hanging out in taverns the way I did back then, swilling beer and bitching about the Dodgers and how they're being destroyed by their greedy owner. I've come full circle, you might say. Me and the Bums, both.

POSSIBILITIES

I HAD BEEN in the backyard no more than two minutes when Roger Telford's bald head popped up above the boundary fence. It was hardly a surprise. Very little that goes on in my neighborhood escapes notice by Telford and his wife Aileen. To merely call them nosy neighbors would be to do them an injustice. They are the quintessential, prototypical poster children for nosy neighbors—sly, sneaky, suspicious, intrusive, rude, and annoying in the extreme.

"I thought I heard snuffling and growling noises over there," he said. "Don't tell me Suzanne has let you buy a dog."

"All right," I said, "I won't."

"*Is* that mutt yours?"

"He's not a mutt. He's a Rottweiler mix. He belongs to the Lindemans, next block over."

"Well, it's a good thing he doesn't belong to you. Aileen and I don't like dogs, especially big dogs. Messy. Always digging things up. Bark all the damn time."

"George doesn't bark much."

"George? How do you know his name?"

"It's on his collar tag."

"Well, it's a stupid name for a mutt. What's he doing in your yard?"

"Visiting," I said. "There's a loose board in our back fence that I haven't gotten around to fixing yet."

"What's that he's chewing on?"

"Well, it looks like a bone . . . yes, by golly, that's what it is all right. A bone."

"Damn big one. I don't think I've ever seen a bone quite like that. He carry it in with him?"

"No. I gave it to him."

"*You* did? Where'd you get a bone like that?"

"Out of our freezer."

His face wrinkled into an expression resembling a contemplative basset hound's. Telford likes to believe he is a deep thinker. His wife likes to believe she is too. They labor under this self-deception because they're both writers of a sort. He concocts texts on how to fix this or that around the house and she writes cookbooks, her magnum opus being *The Sublime Purple Vegetable: Eggplant Delicacies from Around the World.* They both work at home, giving them ample opportunity to pursue their alternate joint career of meddling in other people's business.

"Is that where all those packages came from, too?" he asked at length.

"What packages?"

"Jammed into your trash can this morning."

"Roger, I'm surprised at you. You usually employ more subtle means of snooping than pawing through garbage cans."

"It wasn't me doing the pawing," he said indignantly. "It was one of those other damn neighborhood mutts. Caught it dragging one of the packages out when I rolled my own can out for pick up. I chased it off and put the package back into your can. That's when I happened to notice all the others."

"Very good," I said. "Very inventive. You ought to give fiction writing a try."

"It happens to be the truth. So why did you throw out all that good meat?"

"It wasn't good. Not anymore. Venison, mostly, that one of my coworkers gave us last year."

"What was wrong with it?"

"Freezer burn," I said.

"What?"

"It's a phenomenon that takes place when you leave things in the freezer too long. Surely you've come across references to it while researching those books you write."

"I know what freezer burn is. But the packages I saw were mostly thawed."

"Well, of course they were. I took them out of the freezer and put them into the trash can last night. All except the bone for George. Freezer burn doesn't bother him."

Telford did his basset hound impression again. To avoid watching him at his mental labors, I looked up at the sky. It was a nice evening, clear but a little too crisp to sit out on the porch and read. I sighed. Autumn was almost here. The leaves on the maple tree were already starting to turn.

"What was all that noise coming from your place last night?" Telford demanded. He never asks; he always demands. "You don't make noise like that cleaning out a freezer. Late, too—went on until after eleven. Sounded like power tools."

"It was," I said. "I was working in the basement."

"Doing what?"

"Completing a project."

"What kind of project?"

"A private kind."

"Big secret," Telford said peevishly. "You had the shades closed over the basement windows. Matter of fact, you've had most of your curtains and shades drawn the past couple of days."

"Must have been frustrating for you, not being able to look in with your binoculars."

"You think I'd spy on you with binoculars?"

"I know you would. I've seen you doing it."

He made a noise in his throat not unlike the one George had made when I had given him the bone. "Damn late to be using power tools," he said. "Kept Aileen and me awake. Must've kept Suzanne awake, too."

"I doubt it."

"Oh? Why not?"

"She wasn't here."

"What do you mean, she wasn't here?"

George seemed to have grown as bored with the conversation as I had. He'd been lying on the grass with the bone propped between his forepaws, gnawing on it. Now he stood up, took a firmer grip with his teeth, shook himself, and trotted off toward the back fence.

"Well, Howard?"

"Well what?"

"What'd you mean, Suzanne wasn't here last night?"

"Just what I said. She's not here today, either. That's why George was allowed to visit and why I felt free to give him the bone, in case you're wondering."

"Where is she? Where'd she go?"

"Away," I said.

"Away? When? Where?"

"Two days ago. On a trip."

"The hell you say. I was home all day Sunday. Aileen and I were both home, and we didn't see either of you leave."

"I know you try to keep tabs on everything that goes on over here, Roger, but now and then you do miss something. Now if you don't mind, I have things to do in the house."

He called something after me, but I closed my ears to it. Silence and privacy, in my neighborhood and on my property, are rare and precious states to be retreated into with all dispatch whenever possible.

I was in Suzanne's bedroom closet, taking articles of her clothing off hangers and folding them into Teflon bags, when the telephone rang. Aileen Telford, predictably enough.

"Howard," she said in her nasal voice, "where's Suzanne?"

"Suzanne is away. As Roger has no doubt told you by now."

"Well, I need to talk to her. A question for my new book of parsnip recipes. Where did she go?"

"She's visiting."

"Visiting who? Where?"

"Her sister, if you must know. She's been ill."

"Suzanne is ill?"

I sighed. "Not Suzanne. Her sister."

"I didn't know Suzanne had a sister. She never mentioned her to me."

"She seldom speaks of her. They've never been close."

"Then why did she go visit her?"

"I just explained why. Her sister is ill. Family duty."

"When will she be back?"

"I don't know. It might be a while. A long while."

There was a deep-thinking pause before Aileen said, "Where does her sister live?"

"Duluth. That's in Minnesota."

"I know where Duluth is. What's her sister's name and phone number?"

"I can't tell you that."

"What? Why can't you?"

"Suzanne doesn't want to be disturbed. She doesn't want her sister disturbed. You calling her up would qualify as a disturbance."

Another pause. At length she said in sepulchral tones, "Howard, I don't mind saying that Roger and I are a little concerned."

"About Suzanne's sister?"

"About Suzanne."

"Why should you be concerned about Suzanne?"

"All sorts of funny things seem to have been going on over there the past few days. That's why."

"You think so? Define funny."

"You know what I mean. You can't blame us for wondering—"

"Can't I?" I said, and hung up on her.

When I came out through the front door with another cardboard carton, Telford was standing at the base of the porch steps. More accurately, he was hopping at the base of the steps from one foot to the other as if he had to go to the bathroom. I had witnessed this behavior many times before. Coupled with the gaudy yellow sweatsuit he was wearing, it meant that he was about to head off on his morning jog-and-snoop around the neighborhood.

"What's all this, Howard?" He waved a hand at my car in the driveway, the back seat and trunk of which I had already filled with other cartons and plastic bags. "You're not moving out, are you?"

"And deprive you of a prime surveillance object? No such luck."

"What's in all those boxes and bags?"

"What do you suppose is in them?"

"Looks like it might be clothing and stuff."

"Brilliant deduction," I said. "Clothing and stuff is what it is."

"What're you planning to do with it?"

"What I usually do with rummage. Take it to Goodwill."

"Rummage, eh? Seems like a lot."

"It is a lot. Obviously."

I carried the last carton to the car and put it on the passenger seat. Telford followed, still hopping.

"Mostly your stuff?" he asked then.

"No. As a matter of fact, it's mostly Suzanne's."

That produced a frown. "How come?"

"How come what?"

"How come it's mostly her things you're getting rid of?"

"She doesn't have any use for them any longer."

"What does that mean?"

"It means she no longer has any use for them."

"Why doesn't she?"

"You'll have to ask her when she gets home."

"I'm asking you."

"You'll be leaving frustrated, then. My answer is that it's none of your business."

Telford showed up again that afternoon, shortly after I returned home. I'd left Howard J. Bennett & Associates, Income Tax Spe-

cialists—i.e., one hardworking CPA and two junior partners—
early to do some shopping. I was unloading the trunk of the car,
with the garage door still open, when all of a sudden there he was
breathing down my neck. Quick and silent, like a sneaky ghost.

"What's that you've got there?" he said. "Is that paint?"

"Your ratiocinative powers are amazing. Did you deduce the
contents from the words 'White Latex Paint' on the can, or was it
some other clue?"

"What're you going to paint?"

"My workshop, if you must know."

"Didn't look like it needed painting, the last time I saw it."

"Well, it does now. There are marks on two of the walls."

"Marks?"

"You know—nicks, scrapes, stains."

His eyes narrowed. "What kind of stains?"

"Now what kind of stains would there be on workroom walls?"

"You tell me."

"Splatters of wood sealant, varnish, that sort of thing. You can't
do woodworking without splattering now and then."

"Splattering," he repeated, as if it were a nasty word.

I took the other item I'd purchased out of the trunk and closed
the lid.

"What's that?" Telford said.

"Well, now, let's see. It's shaped like a bowling bag, it's the
size of a bowling bag, and it even resembles a bowling bag. Could
it be a bowling bag?"

"You don't bowl."

"How do you know I don't?"

"You've never said anything about it. And I've never seen you
with any bowling equipment before."

"I used to bowl regularly before I met Suzanne. She thinks it's
a silly game."

"So do I. Where are your ball and shoes?"

"I haven't bought those yet."

"Then how come you bought a bag?"

"I liked the looks of this one."

"Seems ordinary to me. How come you decided to start bowling again?"

"For the exercise."

"In spite of what Suzanne thinks, is that it?"

"She doesn't have a say in the matter."

"Why doesn't she?"

"Because she doesn't," I said.

At a few minutes past midnight, I switched off the living room lights and went to peer around a corner of the side window curtain. The Telford house, as much of it as I could see looming above the boundary Fence, was completely dark.

I gathered up the parcel I'd prepared, made my way through the kitchen to the utility porch, and let myself out into the backyard. The night was clear. There was no moon, but the stars were bright enough to enable me to navigate. I crossed to the gardening shed, removed a spade, and carried it into the rose garden. In the shadows between two of the larger bushes—a pure white damascena and an orange Floribunda, two of Suzanne's favorites—I dug a hole in the soft earth, fairly deep, and buried the parcel. Then I replaced the spade and hurried back to the house.

I wasn't absolutely sure, but when I glanced at the Telford house I thought I detected movement behind the open window to their upstairs bedroom.

The next day was Telford-free, miraculously enough, until six o'clock. I was out front then, watering the lawn, when Aileen appeared, out for her daily constitutional. Roger had his morning jog-and-snoop around the neighborhood, she had her evening walk-and-snoop. You had to admire their methods, the well-coordinated way in which they covered their territory, marching off at different times of the day in different directions to bother people, like a crack stealth commando team.

She came my way in her quick, choppy gait and stopped on the sidewalk a few feet from where I stood. If her husband resembled a basset hound, Aileen's breed was fox terrier—small and wiry with angular features and a long, quivery nose that always seemed moist and shiny, perfect for poking into places it didn't belong.

"Well, Howard," she said, "I don't suppose you've heard from Suzanne."

"But I have. She called last night."

"Did she? And how is her sister's health?"

"Improving."

"So then she'll be coming home soon."

"Possibly not," I said.

The long nose twitched. "Why not, if she isn't needed in Duluth?"

"She may be staying on there just the same."

"For how long?"

"Indefinitely."

"What's that? She's never coming back?"

"Indefinitely doesn't mean never, Aileen."

"Why would she stay in Duluth?"

"She likes it there. More than she likes me, I'm sorry to say."

"Are you trying to tell me she's left you?"

"I'm not trying to tell you anything."

Another twitch. A scowl. "I don't believe Suzanne would give up her home, everything she owns, on a sudden whim. That's not like her."

"I didn't say it was sudden."

"I still don't believe it."

"You don't know her as well as you think you do. Or me, either."

"Well, in your case, that's for sure."

She turned and strode off, muttering, "I knew it. I knew it!" just loud enough for me to hear.

I finished watering, then sat on the porch steps to bask in the evening quiet. I hadn't been there five minutes when the other Telford came marching up my front walk. Direct assault mission, it turned out—an unusual tactic for him.

"Up late again last night, weren't you, Bennett?" he said without preamble.

"So it's Bennett instead of Howard now, is it?"

"*Very* late. Long after midnight."

"If I was," I said, "you and Aileen must've been, too. Just a couple of night owls."

"What were you up to, digging in your rose garden so damn late?"

I raised an eyebrow. "Binoculars weren't enough for you, is that it? Now you've gone high tech and bought an infrared scope for better night spying?"

"You didn't answer my question."

"No, and I'm not going to. What I do on my own property day or night is no one's business but my own."

He sputtered noisily, like a faulty gas-powered lawn-mower. "You won't get away with it, Bennett."

"Get away with what?"

"We'll see to that, one way or another. We'll get to the bottom of this."

"Will you?" I smiled at him. "I like puzzles myself. Great time-passers."

"Puzzles?"

"Sifting through all the many possibilities, looking for pieces that fit together to form the true picture. Very stimulating, mentally."

"I don't know what you're talking about."

"No," I said, "of course you don't."

"More rummage for Goodwill?"

Morning. My open garage. And the Telford fox terrier at it again.

"That's right, Aileen," I said. "More rummage for Goodwill."

"All of it Suzanne's, I suppose."

"You can suppose anything you like."

"Getting rid of everything of hers. Because you claim she's not coming back."

"I made no such claim."

"I don't believe she went to Duluth. I'll bet she doesn't even have a sister."

"A bet you'd lose. She did and she does."

"So you say."

"And what do you say, Aileen?"

She jabbed an accusatory finger at me. "I say she never left. I say you did something to her."

"Such as what?"

"Something unspeakable. You won't get away with it."

"Roger implied the same thing last night."

I placed the last of the Teflon sacks in the trunk of the car. That left only the bowling bag. Aileen seemed to notice it for the first time. Her nose twitched and her teeth snapped together.

"That bag," she said. "What have you got in there?"

"It's a bowling bag. So there must be a bowling ball inside."

"You told Roger you didn't own a ball."

"Did I? He must have misunderstood."

I picked up the bag by its handles, hefting it.

Aileen gasped and drew back. "That stain on the side. It looks . . . *wet.*"

I said, "You're imagining things," and swung the bag inside the trunk.

Another gasp, louder.

"Now what's the matter?"

"It didn't thump when you put it down. It . . . it . . . ."

"It what?"

"Squished"

"Bowling balls don't squish, Aileen."

"I know what I heard!" She was backing away now, her hands up as if to ward off an attack. Her face had assumed the color of the flesh of her favorite sublime vegetable. Her eyes literally bulged.

"Now what could I have in a bowling bag," I said, "that would make a squishing sound?"

She said something that sounded like "Gaahh!" and fled.

The doorbell rang at seven that evening. Two men in business suits stood on the porch outside, one dark and heavy-set, the other fair and loose-coupled. The dark one said, "Mr. Howard Bennett?"

"Yes? What can I do for you?"

"Police officers." They held up badges in leather cases. "My name is Pilofsky. This is Detective Jenkins. We'd like a few words with you, if you don't mind."

"Not at all," I said, "though I can't imagine why."

"All right if we come inside?"

I led them into the living room. Jenkins said, "We'll get right to the point, Mr. Bennett. We've had a report of suspicious activity concerning you and your wife."

"Ah," I said. "Now I understand. The Telfords. I should have known they would call you."

"Why is that?"

"They're the people for whom the phrase 'neighbors from hell' was coined. Sneaks and snoops of the worst sort, and melodramatic to boot. They've been insufferable since Suzanne was called away unexpectedly several days ago."

"Where is your wife, Mr. Bennett?" Pilofsky asked.

"Visiting her bedridden sister in Duluth. I told the Telfords that more than once."

"Is she coming back?"

"Of course. As soon as her sister's condition improves."

"Mrs. Telford claims you told her your wife was leaving you and staying in Duluth permanently."

"Then she misunderstood me. Just as both of them have persisted in misunderstanding a series of perfectly innocent incidents."

"Suppose you give us your version of those incidents."

I obliged at some length. Jenkins took notes.

Pilofsky said, "You didn't address the issue of the 'wet and squishy' bowling bag."

"Oh, that. Aileen Telford has a hyperactive imagination—she's a writer, you know. The bag wasn't wet. It was merely stained. And there was nothing in it except an old bowling ball of mine. She heard what she wanted to hear when I set it down."

"Where are the bag and ball now?"

"They went to Goodwill with the other rummage," I lied. Actually I had pitched the bag into an industrial dumpster not far from my office when no one was looking.

Both of them nodded and Jenkins made another note.

"So you see," I said, "it's all just a tempest in a teapot."

"So it would seem," Pilofsky said.

"Be all right if we had a look around?" Jenkins asked. "It's your privilege to say no, naturally. We don't have a search warrant." The implication here, of course, was that they could just go get one if they felt it necessary.

"More than all right," I said. "Be my guests. I have nothing to hide."

I conducted them through the house, top to bottom. They were polite and respectful, but quite thorough in their probings. They exhibited particular interest in my newly painted workshop and the rest of the basement, examining my tools and even looking inside the big Amana freezer. Naturally they found nothing incriminating. There was nothing for them to find.

From the basement I took them outside, where I unearthed the hideous ceramic bird sculpture I had buried in the rose garden. "I did it on a whim," I said. "I've always hated that sculpture, and with Suzanne away . . . well, I just couldn't stand to look at it any longer."

"Why bury it?" Pilofsky asked. "Why not just chuck it in the trash?"

I said sheepishly, "To be frank, I was covering my backside. I thought that if Suzanne noticed the sculpture was missing and became upset, I could always dig it up and pretend it had been misplaced." I sighed. "Now that I have dug it up, I suppose I might as well put it back where it belongs. It was a foolish notion to begin with."

Before they left, Jenkins asked for the name, address, and phone number of Suzanne's sister in Duluth. I provided the information, saying, "Please don't call her there unless it's absolutely necessary. I'm sure you understand."

"We just need it for our report, Mr. Bennett."

"Then you're satisfied that this has all been a misunderstanding?"

"Not to mention a waste of the taxpayers' time and money."

"I suppose it's too much to hope that the Telfords will be satisfied too."

"If we are," Pilofsky said meaningfully, "they'd better be."

Neither member of the Snoop Couple bothered me the next day or the morning of the one following. I saw neither hide nor hair of either of them, in fact. But that only meant that they had changed their tactics from overt to covert. They wouldn't be satisfied, no matter what the police had said to them, until they saw Suzanne, hale and hearty, with their own eyes.

Which is why, on the following morning, I drove off whistling.

The three P.M. flight from Duluth was on time. Suzanne was waiting with her bag when I pulled up to the curb at Arrivals, scowling at her watch even though I wasn't even a minute late.

On the way out of the airport I said, "It's good to have you home, dear."

"Horse apples," she said. Her favorite epithet, and one I've always loathed. "You were probably wishing I'd stayed away a lot longer."

"That's not true."

"Of course it's true. Well, you may get your wish. If my sister's condition doesn't improve over the next week or so, I'll probably have to go back there again."

"I'm sorry to hear that," I said.

"Horse apples. Don't try to deny you've liked living alone. All that freedom to stick your nose in a book and neglect your chores."

"I've never neglected my chores."

"Not when I'm around to prod you into doing them. I don't suppose you did everything on the list I gave you?"

"Ah, but I did."

"Finished building the new table for my sewing room?

"In one evening."

"Took everything on my rummage list to Goodwill?"

"Yes, dear. Plus some odds and ends from the basement."

"Painted that ugly workshop of yours?"

"All four walls."

"Cleaned out the pantry and the freezer?"

"And the refrigerator. A good thing I did, too. There was a honeydew melon hidden in back that we bought weeks ago and forgot about."

"It must've been rotten."

"It was," I said. "Squishy, in fact."

"Mmm," she said. "Did you do anything else besides loaf?"

"Oh, I had some fun with the Telfords."

"Fun? With those busybodies?"

"We played a game."

"What kind of game?"

"Actually, it was one they made up. I never would have thought of it myself. But I learned the rules quickly and even invented a few of my own."

"Mmm. Who won?"

"I did."

"How nice for you," she said, and let the subject drop. She never has had any interest in my small triumphs.

When we arrived home, I made a point of parking prominently in the middle of the driveway and helping Suzanne out of the car. The Telfords had been sitting on their porch. They both scrambled to their feet when they saw her, their necks craning, looking like a pair of ungainly, agitated geese. I waved at them cheerfully. They ducked into their house without even waving back.

After I finished the dinner dishes, I sat on the front porch to watch dusk settle over the neighborhood. The evening was warmish and dusk is my favorite part of the day—quiet, peaceful, a contemplative time. Lights showed in the Telford house, but there was no sign of either Roger or Aileen. For the first time in as long as I could remember, all their window curtains were drawn and none of them were fluttering at the corners. It would be a good long while, if ever, I thought, before they resumed their spying on the Bennett household. After years of abuse, the prospect of protracted peace and privacy was a heady one.

The screen door banged after awhile and Suzanne came out to plop down next to me. "Why are you grinning?" she demanded.

"Was I grinning? I didn't realize it."

"What were you thinking about?"

"Oh, this and that. Possibilities."

"I don't understand you, Howard. Sometimes I wonder what possessed me to marry you in the first place."

Before I could frame a response, George, the Lindemans' Rottweiler mix, came trotting around the corner of the house. Suzanne let out a little screech that caused the dog to stop and flatten slightly with his ears back.

"Howard!"

"Don't worry," I said. "He's harmless."

"Harmless? An ugly brute like that? How did he get into our yard?"

"There's a loose board in the back fence—"

"Loose board? Why haven't you fixed it? What's the matter with you? A beast like that, running loose. There's no telling what kind of damage he'll do. Get rid of him this instant!"

I got up and went down the porch steps. George's tail began to wag. He came over and licked my hand.

"And don't come back until you've fixed that board. Do you hear me?"

"Yes, dear. You don't need to shout."

"Horse apples," she said. She went back inside and slammed the door behind her.

I said, "Come on, George," and led the dog around back and across the yard. He didn't want to leave. He stood looking up at me with round, eager eyes, his tongue lolling. I leaned down and patted his head.

"I don't have anything for you tonight, boy," I told him. "But I might have something in the foreseeable future. You never know. Life is full of possibilities."

Then I shooed him out and went to get my tools so I could pretend to fix the loose board in the fence.

OUT BEHIND THE SHED

There was a dead guy behind the parts shed.

I went out there to get a Ford oil pan for Barney and I saw him lying on his back in the weedy grass. He didn't have a face. There was blood and bone and pulp and black scorch marks where his face used to be. I couldn't even guess if he was anybody I knew.

I stood there shivering. It was cold . . . Jesus, it was cold for late March. The sky was all glary, like the sun coming off a sheet-metal roof. Only there wasn't any sun. Just a shiny silver overcast, so cold-hot bright it hurt your eyes to look at it. The wind was big and gusty, the kind that burns right through clothing and puts a rash like frostbite on your skin. No matter what I'd done all day I couldn't seem to get warm.

I'd known right off, as soon as I got out of bed, that it was going to be a bad day. The cold and the funny bright sky was one thing. Another was Madge. She'd started in on me about money again even before she made the coffee. How we were barely making ends meet and couldn't even afford to get the TV fixed, and why couldn't I find a better-paying job or let her go to work part-time or at least take a second job myself, nights, to bring in a little extra. The same old song and dance. The only old tune she hadn't played was the one about how much she ached for another kid before she got too old, as if two wasn't enough.

Then I came in here to work and Barney was in a grumpy mood on account of a head cold and the fact that we hadn't had three new repair jobs in a week. Maybe he'd have to do some retrenching if things didn't pick up pretty soon, he said. That was the word he used, retrenching. Laying me off was what he meant. I'd been working for him five years, steady, never missed a day sick, never screwed up on a single job, and he was thinking about firing me. What would I do then? Thirty-six years old, wife and two kids, house mortgaged to the hilt, no skills except auto mechanic and nobody hiring mechanics right now. What the hell would I do?

Oh, it was a bad day, all right. I hadn't thought it could get much worse, but now I knew that it could.

Now there was this dead guy out here behind the shed.

I ran back inside the shop. Barney was still banging away under old Mrs. Cassell's Ford, with his legs sticking out over the end of the roller cart. I yelled at him to slide out. He did and I said, "Barney . . . Barney, there's a dead guy out by the parts shed."

He said, "You trying to be funny?"

"No," I said. "No kidding and no lie. He's out there in the grass behind the shed."

"Another of them derelicts come in on the freights, I suppose. You sure he's dead? Maybe he's just passed out."

"*Dead,* Barney. I know a dead guy when I see one."

He hauled up on his feet. He was a big Swede, five inches and fifty pounds bigger than me, and he had a way of looming over you that made you feel even smaller. He looked down into my face and then scowled and said in a different voice, "Froze to death?"

"No," I said. "He hasn't got a face anymore. His face is all blown away."

"Jesus. Somebody killed him, you mean?"

"Somebody must of. Who'd do a thing like that, Barney? Out behind our shed?"

He shook his head and cracked one of his big gnarly knuckles. The sound echoed like a gunshot in the cold garage. Then, without saying anything else, he swung around and fast-walked out through the rear door.

I didn't go with him. I went over and stood in front of the wall heater. But I still couldn't get warm. My shoulders kept hunching up and down inside my overalls and I couldn't feel my nose or ears or the tips of my fingers, as if they weren't there anymore. When I looked at my hands they were all red and chapped, like Madge's hands after she's been washing clothes or dishes. They twitched a little, too; the tendons were like worms wiggling under a handkerchief.

Pretty soon Barney came back. He had a funny look on his moon face but it wasn't the same kind he'd had when he went out. He said, "What the hell, Joe? I got no time for games and neither do you."

"Games?"

"There's nobody behind the shed," he said.

I stared at him. Then I said, "In the grass, not ten feet past the far corner."

"I looked in the grass," Barney said. His nose was running from the cold. He wiped it off on the sleeve of his overalls. "I looked all over. There's no dead guy. There's nobody."

"But I saw him. I swear to God."

"Well, he's not there now."

"Somebody must of come and dragged him off, then."

"Who'd do that?"

"Same one who killed him."

"There's no blood or nothing," Barney said. He was back to being grumpy. His voice had that hard edge and his eyes had a squeezed look. "None of the grass is even flattened down. You been seeing things, Joe."

"I tell you, it was the real thing."

"And I tell *you,* it wasn't. Go out and take another look, see for yourself. Then get that oil pan out of the shed and your ass back to work. I promised old lady Cassell we'd have her car ready by five-thirty."

I went outside again. The wind had picked up a couple of notches, turned even colder; it was like fire against my bare skin. The hills east of town were all shimmery with haze, like in one of those desert mirages. There was a tree smell in the air but it wasn't the usual good pine-and-spruce kind. It was a eucalyptus smell, even though there weren't any eucalyptus trees within two miles of here. It made me think of cat piss.

I put my head down and walked slow over to the parts shed. And stopped just as I reached it to draw in a long breath. And then went on to where I could see past the far corner.

The dead guy was there in the grass. Lying right where I'd seen him before, laid out on his back with one leg drawn up and his face blown away.

The wind gusted just then, and when it did it made sounds like howls and moans. I wanted to cover my ears. Cover my eyes, too, to keep from seeing what was in the grass. But I didn't do either one. All I did was stand there shivering with my eyes wide open, trying to blink away some of the shimmery haze that seemed to have crawled in behind them. Nothing much was clear now, inside or out—nothing except the dead guy.

"Joe!"

Barney, somewhere behind me. I didn't turn around but I did back up a couple of steps. Then I backed up some more, until I was past the corner and couldn't see the dead guy anymore. Then I swung around and ran to where Barney was in the shop doorway.

"He's there, Barney, he's there, he's there—"

He gave me a hard crack on the shoulder. It didn't hurt; only the cold hurt where it touched my face and hands. He said, "Get hold of yourself, man."

"I *swear* it," I said, "right where I saw him before."

"All right, take it easy."

"I don't know how you missed seeing him," I said. I pulled at his arm. "I'll show you, come on."

I kept tugging on him and finally he came along, grumbling. I led the way out behind the shed. The dead guy was still there, all right. I blew out the breath I'd been holding and said, "Didn't I tell you? Didn't I?"

Barney stared down at the dead guy. Then he stared at me with his mouth open a little and his nose dripping snot. He said, "I don't see anything."

"You don't . . . what?"

"Grass, just grass."

"What's the matter with you? You're looking right at him!"

"The hell I am. The only two people out here are you and me."

I blinked and blinked and shook my head and blinked some more but the dead guy didn't go away. He was *there*. I started to bend over and touch him, to make absolutely sure, but I couldn't do it. He'd be cold, as cold as the wind—colder. I couldn't stand to touch anything that cold and dead.

"I've had enough of this," Barney said.

I made myself look at him instead of the dead guy. The cat-piss smell had gotten so strong I felt like gagging.

"He's there," I said, pleading. "Oh God, Barney, can't you see him?"

"There's nobody there. How many times do I have to say it? You better go on inside, Joe. Both of us better. It's freezing out here." He put a hand on my arm but I shook it off. That made him mad. "All right," he said, "if that's the way you want it. How about if I call Madge? Or maybe Doc Kiley?"

"No," I said.

"Then quit acting like a damn fool. Get a grip on yourself, get back to work. I mean it, Joe. Any more of this crap and you'll regret it."

"No," I said again. "You're lying to me. That's it, isn't it? You're lying to me."

"Why would I lie to you?"

"I don't know, but that's what you're doing. Why don't you want me to believe he's there?"

"Goddamn it, *there's nobody there!*"

Things just kept happening today—bad things one right after another, things that made no sense. The cold, Madge, Barney, the dead guy, the haze, the cat-piss smell, Barney again—and now a cold wind chilling me inside as well as out, as if icy gusts had blown right in through my flesh and were howling and prowling around my heart. I'd never felt like this before. I'd never been this cold or this scared or this frantic.

I pulled away from Barney and ran back into the shop and into the office and unlocked the closet and took out the duck gun he lets me keep in there because Madge don't like guns in the house. When I got back to the shed, Barney was just coming out with a Ford oil pan in his gnarly hands. His mouth pinched up tight and his eyes got squinty when he saw me.

He said, "What the hell's the idea bringing that shotgun out here?"

"Something's going on," I said, "something crazy. You see that dead guy there or don't you?"

"You're the one who's crazy, Joe. Give me that thing before somebody gets hurt."

He took a step toward me. I backed up and leveled the duck gun at him. "Tell me the truth," I said, desperate now, "tell me you see him lying there!"

He didn't tell me. Instead he gave a sudden lunge and got one hand on the barrel and tried to yank the gun away and oh Jesus him pulling on it like that made me jerk the trigger. The load of birdshot hit him full on and he screamed and the wind screamed with him and then he stopped but the wind didn't. Inside and out, the wind kept right on screaming.

I stood looking down at him lying in the grass with one leg drawn up and his face blown away. I could see him clear, even through that shimmery haze. Just him down there. Nobody else.

Just Barney.

TOILING IN THE FIELDS
OF THE LORD

THE HARVEST was almost done. One more week, maybe only a few days, and all the lettuce would be picked, the fields would be bare earth again.

It had been very hot this day, the hottest of the long season, and the air had cooled little since nightfall. I sat resting beneath the lamplit front window of my trailer. An old man's bones ache in weather like this, from all the stooping and straightening and the slashing strokes of the lettuce knife. I was still strong enough to toil in the fields, do the Lord's work, but for how much longer?

This was not a good thought and I put it out of my mind.

From the other end of the camp, the loud pagan music of the young people rose and fell and there were shouts and laughter. Angry voices, too, from both men and women. Nerves fray, tempers grow short, passions flare in the heat of summer. There had been two fights and much growling and name-calling in the fields today. Tonight, more of the same.

The camp sounds were of no interest to me. I listened to the throb of the crickets, the call of nightbirds in the willows that lined the river bank below. Here alone beneath the star-bright sky, I was at peace.

But I was not alone for long. Soon Rosa Caldera appeared, as she did almost every night, in one of her thin, tight dresses with nothing beneath it. Young, wild, filled with sin and mischief. Another like Corinne. She might have been Corrine, forty years ago. I knew them so well, the Corrines and Rosas, the other wicked ones in the fields and camps.

Rosa stopped, as she always did, and said in her teasing voice, "Hello, grandfather. Hot night, eh?"

"Yes. Very hot."

"Cooler down by the river. Cooler *in* the river."

I said nothing.

"I think I'll go swimming. Will you come down later and watch me?"

"No."

"Ah, but you will. I've seen you watching me before."

I said nothing.

"Why don't you come swimming with me tonight? No one else will be there. We'll swim naked together."

"No."

"You're too old, eh? Too old to do anything but watch."

I said nothing.

"Well, *abuelo*?" she said, and laughed, and winked at me. "What do you say?"

"God will punish you for your sins."

She laughed again. "That's what you always say. Why don't you think up something new?"

She walked away, laughing, swinging her hips. Once, she looked back over her shoulder and stuck her tongue out at me. More laughter flowed back from her as she disappeared into the darkness.

I sat listening to the crickets and the nightbirds, wishing for a cool breeze. None came. What came were the two boys, Pete Simms and Miguel Santos, as they, too, did almost every night. Young like Rosa, their backs strong but their minds small and mean, their hearts cold. One was fat, the other thin, and both were ugly of face. They took much pleasure in deviling me because it gave them a sense of power. The young ones like Rosa would have nothing to do with them.

"Hey, there, Harry," Pete said. "How's it hanging tonight?"

I said nothing.

"It don't hang on Harry no more," Miguel said. "You get to be his age, it shrivels up and hides. Ain't that right, old man?"

I said nothing.

"Oh, Christ, it's hot. Don't the heat never bother you?"

"No."

"Nothing much bothers you, seems like."

"A man lives long enough," I said, "he learns patience."

"Don't worry, be happy. Right?"

"Yes. Don't worry, be happy. Do what has to be done."

"Like what? Picking lettuce for crappy wages?"

"Yes. Working in the fields."

"You always been a farm worker, Harry? I mean, you ever do anything else?"

"No. Nothing else."

Miguel laughed. "So you was born to it. Born migrant worker, born *bracero.*"

"Every man is born to do one good thing with his life," I said.

"And you think picking lettuce is yours?"

"Toiling in the fields is honest work. The Lord's work."

They both laughed this time, like donkeys braying. "You hear that, Pete? The Lord's work, he calls it. Toiling in the fields of the Lord!"

"You're funny as hell, Harry, you know that? A freakin' laugh riot."

"Man, you really believe what you just said?"

"Yes," I said. "I believe it."

"Then you're crazy. You been working in the hot sun too long."

"*Way* too long," Pete said. "His brain's been fried."

I said nothing. I reached behind my chair, lifted the full quart bottle, broke the seal, and took a small sip. They both watched me with their eyes opened wide.

"Hey," Miguel said, "look at that. The holy roller's got a jug of tequila."

"Yeah. Good stuff, too."

"Never seen you take a drink before, *hombre viejo*. You been holding out on us."

I shrugged my shoulders. "Every now and then, a sip or two, when the harvest is almost done."

"A sip or two. Shit. One bottle prob'ly lasts you the whole season."

"Wouldn't last me one night," Pete said.

"How about letting us have a taste?"

"No. You boys are too young."

They thought this, too, was funny. "Come on, don't be stingy. Just a quick one for each of us, hah?"

"No."

"You better change that to yes," Miguel said. "You wouldn't want to make us mad at you."

"Why should you be mad at me?"

"For holding out on us. For not sharing. If we got mad, why then maybe we'd just have to take that bottle away from you."

"You would do that?"

"What would *you* do if we did, an old fart like you? Holler for help?"

"No."

"Fight us, try to take the bottle back?"

"No."

"So you see? Share and make us all happy."

"Why are you picking on an old man?"

"You're a funny dude, that's why," Pete said. "You make us laugh."

I said nothing.

"Nobody's looking, nobody's around. Give us the bottle, let us have a couple of swallows."

"That's all we want," Miguel said, "just a couple of swallows."

I hesitated, but only for a moment. Then I sighed and held out the bottle. Miguel grabbed it first, drank long and deep until Pete took it away from him. He, too, drank long and deep, smacked his lips and wiped a fat hand across his mouth.

"Man, that's *good!*"

"Strong as goat piss. Whoo."

"I feel like having another one."

"Yeah. Gimme that bottle."

"You boys better not drink too much," I said.

"No? Why's that?"

"Too much tequila does bad things to a man on a hot night."

"What bad things?"

I said nothing.

"He means it makes you horny," Pete said. He punched me on the shoulder. "Isn't that what you mean, Harry?"

I said nothing.

"Bad things," Miguel said, and laughed. "Bet tequila don't do nothing bad to the holy roller except get him a little *borracho.*"

"Hey, old man, we never seen you with a woman. You ever been married?"

"Yes."

"No shit? What was her name?"

"Corrine."

"What happened to her? She die or something?"

I said nothing.

"Maybe she dumped him," Pete said. "That what happened? She dump your ass?"

I said nothing.

"Maybe she run off with somebody else," Miguel said. "How about it, *hombre viejo*? That the way it was?"

"Yes."

"Hah! So she did run off. When was that?"

"Long time ago."

"How long?"

"Forty years."

Pete drank more tequila. "Man, that's just about forever."

"What'd you do?" Miguel asked. "After she run off."

"Nothing. There was nothing to do."

"I know what I'd've done. I'd've gone after her and kicked her ass and busted the dude's head. That's what I'd've done."

I said nothing.

"Forty years," Pete said. "But you ain't been without a woman since, right? You had plenty in your day, huh?"

"No."

"No? What you mean, no?"

"Sins of the flesh," I said.

They both laughed. "Sins of the flesh," Miguel said. He took the bottle from Pete, drank deeply. "That's a hot one, that is. That's funny as hell."

"You trying to tell us you ain't had a woman in forty years? You ain't been laid in all that time?"

"It's the truth."

"What kind of man don't want to get laid for forty years? Huh?"

I said nothing.

"So what you been doing all that time?" Pete said. "Choking your lizard?"

I said nothing.

"He don't even do that," Miguel said. "All he does is pick crops and sit here by himself at night, all tired out from the Lord's work."

"Toiling in the fields of the Lord. Right, Harry?"

"Yes."

They laughed and drank. I listened to the crickets and the nightbirds and wished for a small breeze. It was very hot.

"Damn," Miguel said, "I'm getting a heat on."

"Oh, yeah."

"Getting a hard on, too. How about we go over to Salinas, pick up a couple of *putas*?"

"We ain't been paid yet, remember? We ain't got no money, remember?"

"Hey, Harry, you got any money?"

"No," I said.

"Twenty bucks, that's all we'd need. How about it?"

"I don't have twenty dollars."

"No, huh? No stash in your trailer?"

"No."

"Maybe he's lying," Miguel said. "Maybe we oughta go in, have a look around."

"Go ahead," I said. "You won't find any money."

"Oh, shit, forget it," Pete said. "He ain't lying to us. All he's got is this jug of the best damn tequila. And he wouldn't mind if we was to go ahead and finish it, ain't that right, old man?"

I said nothing.

"I tell you," Miguel said, slurring his words now, "this tequila makes me horny as hell. Harry here don't need pussy but I do. Man, real bad!"

"Forget it. Ain't nobody in the camp gonna give it to you."

"Rosa Caldera might."

Pete laughed so hard he choked. "Rosa Caldera! That bitch! She wouldn't let you screw her if you was the last dude on the planet."

"Plenty of guys've had her."

"Sure, but not you. Not either of us, man."

"She came by here a few minutes ago," I said.

They squinted at me. "Who did?" Pete said.

"Rosa Caldera. On her way to the river."

"Yeah? Who was with her?"

"No one. She was alone."

"So she was going to the river," Miguel said. "What for?"

"To swim naked under the willows by the sandbar."

". . . Naked? How the hell you know that? She tell you that?"

"I know," I said.

"She wouldn't tell him nothing like that," Pete said. "He must've seen her. That right, Harry? You seen Rosa swimming naked in the river?"

"Yes."

Pete laughed. "Hey, he's a peeper. A peeping holy roller."

Miguel didn't laugh. "She goes there alone? Swims alone?"

"Tonight, yes. But not always."

"Who else swims with her?"

"Men. Different men."

"They get naked too?"

"Yes. Sometimes."

"What else they do besides swim, huh?"

I said nothing.

"Screw? Rosa screw guys down there in the river?"

I said nothing.

"Sure she does," Pete said. "And Harry watches. You like to watch, huh, old man?"

"No."

"Yeah, sure you do. You keep going back, right? That's how you know about the guys Rosa screws down there."

I said nothing.

Miguel drank again, licked his lips. "She went down there alone tonight, you said."

"Yes. Alone."

"Maybe she's meeting some dude later," Pete said.

"No. Not tonight."

"How you know that?"

"She asked me to swim with her."

"The hell she did!"

"She didn't mean it. She was teasing me."

"Yeah, Rosa the cockteaser."

"How long she stay down there in the river?" Miguel asked.

"A long time on hot nights."

"Under the willows by the sandbar—that's where she swims?"

"Yes."

They looked at each other. Again they drank. Their eyes were very bright in the pale light from my trailer window.

"Harry," Pete said, "you're too damn old to be drinking tequila on a hot night like this, so we're gonna do you a favor—we're gonna take this bottle away so you won't be tempted. What you say to that?"

I said nothing.

Pete laughed again, but Miguel did not, and together they staggered away into the darkness.

Noises woke me, loud voices close by. I pulled on my pants and went outside. It was very late but the camp was alive with movement and bobbing lights, men and women running past my trailer in the direction of the river. I followed them.

Eladio Sachez came hobbling up to me, as excited as I have ever seen him. His sun-weathered face was shiny with sweat.

"Harry," he said, "it's terrible, Harry—isn't it terrible?"

"What is? What's going on?"

"Haven't you heard? Don't you know?"

"No," I said, "I was asleep. What happened?"

"Rosa Caldera's been killed. Raped and killed."

"Raped and killed, you say?"

"Down by the river. Jaime Valdez was out for a walk and heard her scream. She was dead when he found her. Naked, raped, her head crushed with a tequila bottle."

"Do they know who did it?"

"Miguel Santos and Pete Simms," Eladio said. "Jaime saw them running away. But they won't get far, the police will catch them. Isn't it an awful thing, Harry?"

"Yes," I said, "it's an awful thing."

He hobbled away and I went back to my trailer. But I was not sleepy anymore. I walked down to a different part of the river and found a place under one of the willows.

It was cooler there, close to the moon-silvered water. The camp noise was only a low buzzing murmur, all but lost in the throbbing song of the crickets. Peaceful. A man could settle down in a place like this, if he was a settling-down kind of man.

But I was not, and had not been for forty years.

The harvest here in the Salinas Valley had been a good one, but now it was almost finished and soon I would be moving on. To other places, other crops, other fertile fields.

The Lord's work is never done.

THE MONSTER

He was after the children.

Meg knew it, all at once, as soon as he was inside the house. She couldn't have said exactly how she knew. He was pleasant enough on the surface, smiling, friendly. Big and shaggy-haired in his uniform, hairy all over like a bear. But behind his smile and underneath his fur there was menace, evil. She felt it, intuited it—a mother's instinct for danger. He was after Kate and Bobby. One of those monsters who preyed on little children, hurt them, did unspeakable things to them—

"Downstairs or upstairs?" he said.

". . . What?"

"The stopped-up drain. Downstairs here or upstairs?"

A feeling of desperation was growing in her, spreading toward panic. She didn't know what to do. "I think you'd better leave." The words were out before she realized what she was saying.

"Huh? I just got here, Mrs. Thompson. Your husband said you got a stopped-up drain—that's right, isn't it?"

Why did I let him in? she thought. Just because he said Philip sent him, that doesn't make it so. And even if Philip did send him . . . Oh God, why *him,* of all the plumbers in this city?

"No," she said. "No, it . . . it's all right now. It's working again, there's nothing wrong with it."

He wasn't smiling anymore. "You kidding me?"

"Why would I do that?"

"Yeah, why? Over at the door you said you been expecting me, come on in and fix the drain."

"I didn't—"

"You did, lady. Look, I haven't got time to play games. And it's gonna cost you sixty-five bucks whether I do any work or not so you might as well let me take a look."

"It's all right now, I tell you."

"Okay, maybe it is. But if it was stopped-up once today, it could happen again. You never know with the pipes in these old houses. So where is it, up or down?"

"Please . . ."

"Upstairs, right? Yeah, now I think of it, your husband said it was in the upstairs bathroom."

No! The word was like a scream in her mind. The upstairs bathroom was between their room, hers and Philip's, and the nursery. Baby Kate in her crib, not even a year old, and Bobby, just two, napping in his bed . . . so innocent and helpless . . . and this man, this beast—

He moved past her to the stairs, hefting his tool kit in one huge, scab-knuckled hand. "You want to show me where it is?"

"No!" She cried it aloud this time.

"Hey," he said, "you don't have to bust my eardrums." He shook his head the way Philip did sometimes when he was vexed with her. "Well, I can find it myself. Can't hide a bathroom from an old hand like me."

He started up the stairs.

She stood paralyzed, staring in horror as he climbed. She tried to shriek at him to stop, go away, don't hurt the babies, but her voice had frozen in her throat. If any harm came to Kate and Bobby, she could never forgive herself—she would shrivel up and die. So many childless years, all the doctors who'd told her and Philip that she could never conceive, and then the sudden miracle of her first pregnancy and Bobby's birth, the second miracle that was Kate. . . . If she let either of them be hurt she would be as much of a monster as the one climbing the stairs—

Stop him!

The paralysis left her as abruptly as it had come on; her legs pumped, carried her headlong into the kitchen. A knife, the big butcher knife . . . She grabbed it out of the rack, raced back to the stairs.

He was already on the second floor. She couldn't see him, but she could hear his heavy menacing tread in the hallway, going down the hallway.

Toward the nursery.

Toward Kate and Bobby.

She rushed upward, clutching the knife, her terror so immense now it felt as though her head would burst. She ran into the hallway, saw him again—and her heart skipped a beat, the fear ripped inside her like an animal trying to claw its way out of a cage.

He was standing in the nursery doorway, looking in at the children.

She lunged at him with the knife upraised. He turned just before she reached him, and his mouth shaped startled words. But the only sound he made was an explosive grunt when she plunged the knife into his chest.

His mouth flew open; his eyes bulged so wide she thought for an instant they would pop out like seeds from a squeezed orange. One scarred hand plucked at the knife handle. The other groped in her direction, as if to catch and crush her. She leapt back against the far wall, stood huddled against it as he staggered away, still grunting and plucking at the knife handle.

She saw him fall once, lurch upright again, finally reach the top of the stairs; then the grunting ended in a long heaving sigh and he sagged and toppled forward. The sounds he made rolling and bouncing down the stairs were as loud and terrible as the thunder that had terrified her as a child, that still frightened her sometimes on storm-heavy nights.

The noises stopped at last and there was silence.

Meg pushed away from the wall, hurried into the nursery. Bobby, incredibly, was still asleep; he had the face of a golden-haired angel, lying pooched on his side with his tiny arms outstretched. Kate was awake and fussing. Meg picked her up, held her tight, soothed and rocked and murmured to her until the fussing stopped and her tears dried. When the baby was tucked up asleep in her crib, Meg steeled herself and then made her way slowly out to the stairs and down.

The evil one lay crumpled and smeared with red at the bottom. His eyes still bulged, wide open and staring. Dead.

And that was good, it was *good,* because it meant that the children were safe again.

She stepped over him, shuddering, and went to the phone in the kitchen. She called the police first, then Philip at his office to ask him to please come home right away.

A detective sergeant and two uniformed officers arrived first. Meg explained to the detective what had happened, and he seemed very sympathetic. But he was still asking questions when Philip came.

Philip put his strong arms around her, held her; she leaned close to him as always, because he was the only person since her daddy died who had ever made her feel safe. He didn't ask her any questions. He made her sit down in the living room, went with the detective to look at what lay under the sheet at the foot of the stairs.

". . . don't understand it," Philip was saying. "He was highly recommended to me by a friend. Reliable, honest, trustworthy—the best plumber in town."

"Then you did send him over to fix a stopped-up drain."

"Yes. I told my wife I was going to. I just don't understand. Did he try to attack her? Is that why she stabbed him?"

"Not her, no. She said he was after your children. Upstairs in the nursery where they're asleep."

"Oh my God," Philip said.

He must have sensed her standing there because he turned to look at her. I had to do it, Philip, she told him with her eyes. He was a monster and I had to protect the children. Our wonderful son Bobby, sweet baby Kate . . . I'm their mother, I couldn't let them be hurt, could I?

But he didn't believe her. She saw the disbelief in his face before he turned away again, and then she heard him lie to the detective. He lied, he lied, Philip lied—

"We don't have any children," he said.

PUMPKIN

THE PUMPKIN, the strange pumpkin, came into Amanda Sutter's life on a day in late September.

She had spent most of that morning and early afternoon shopping in Half Moon Bay, and it was almost two o'clock when she pointed the old Dodge pickup south on Highway One. She watched for the sign, as she always did; finally saw it begin to grow in the distance, until she could read, first, the bright orange letters that said SUTTER PUMPKIN FARM, and then the smaller black letters underneath: *The Biggest, The Tastiest, The Best— First Prize Winner, Half Moon Bay Pumpkin Festival, 1976.*

Amanda smiled as she turned past the sign, onto the farm's un-paved access road. The wording had been Harley's idea, which had surprised some people who didn't know him very well. Harley was a quiet, reserved man—too reserved, sometimes; she was forever trying to get him to let his hair down a little—and he never bragged. As far as he was concerned, the sign was simply a state-ment of fact. "Well, our pumpkins *are* the biggest, the tastiest, the best," he'd said when one of their neighbors asked him about it. "And we *did* win first prize in 76. If the sign said anything else, it'd be a lie."

That was Harley for you. In a nutshell.

The road climbed up a bare-backed hill, and when she reached the crest Amanda stopped the pickup to admire the view. She never tired of it, especially at this time of year and on this sort of crisp, clear day. The white farm buildings lay in a little pocket directly below, with the fields stretching out on three sides and the ocean vast and empty beyond. The pumpkins were ripe now, the same bright orange as the lettering on the sign—Connecticut Field for the most part, with a single parcel devoted to Small Sugar; hun-dreds of them dotting the brown and green earth like a bonanza of huge gold nuggets, gleaming in the afternoon sun. The sun-glare was caught on the ruffly blue surface of the Pacific, too, so that it likewise carried a sheen of orange-gold.

She sat for a time, watching the Mexican laborers Harley had hired to harvest the pumpkins—to first cut their stems and then, once they had had their two-to-three weeks of curing in the fields, load the bulk of the crop onto produce trucks for shipment to San Francisco and San Jose. It wouldn't be long now before Halloween. And on the weekend preceding it, the annual Pumpkin Festival.

The festival attracted thousands of people from all over the Bay Area and was the year's big doings in Half Moon Bay. There was a parade featuring the high school band and kids dressed up in Halloween costumes; there were booths selling crafts, whole pumpkins, and pumpkin delicacies—pies and cookies, soups and breads; and on Sunday the competition between growers in the area for the season's largest exhibition pumpkin was held. The year Sutter Farm had won the contest, 1976, the fruit Harley had carefully nurtured in a mixture of pure compost and spent-mushroom manure weighed in at 236 pounds. There had been no blue ribbons since, but the prospects seemed good for this season: one of Harley's new exhibition pumpkins had already grown to better than 240 pounds.

Amanda put the Dodge in gear and drove down the road to the farmyard. When she came in alongside the barn she saw Harley talking to one of the laborers, a middle-aged Mexican whose name, she remembered, was Manuel. No, not talking, she realized as she shut off the engine—arguing. She could hear Manuel's raised voice, see the tight, pinched look Harley always wore when he was annoyed or upset.

She went to where they stood. Manuel was saying, "I will not do it, Mr. Sutter. I am sorry, I will not."

"Won't do what?" Amanda asked.

Harley said, "Won't pick one of the pumpkins." His voice was pitched low but the strain of exasperation ran through it. "He says it's haunted."

"What!"

"Not haunted, Mr. Sutter," Manuel said. "No, not that." He turned appealing eyes to Amanda. "This pumpkin must not be picked, *senora.* No one must cut its stem or its flesh, no one must eat it."

"I don't understand, Manuel. Whyever not?"

"There is something . . . I cannot explain it. You must see this pumpkin for yourself. You must . . . feel it."

"Touch it, you mean?"

"No, Mrs. Sutter. *Feel* it."

Harley said, "You've been out in the sun too long, Manuel."

"This is not a joke, *senor*," Manuel said in grave tones. "The other men do not feel it as strongly as I, but they also will not pick this pumpkin. We will all leave if it is cut, and we will not come back."

Amanda felt a vague chill, as if someone had blown a cold breath against the back of her neck. She said, "Where is this pumpkin, Manuel?"

"The east field. Near the line fence."

"Have you seen it, Harley?" she asked her husband.

"Not yet. We might as well go out there, I guess."

"Yes," Manuel said. "Come with me, see for yourself. *Feel* for yourself."

Amanda and Harley got into the pickup; Manuel had driven in from the fields in one of the laborers' flatbed trucks, and he led the way in that. They clattered across the hilly terrain to the field farthest from the farm buildings, to its farthest section near the pole-and-barbed-wire line fence. From there, Manuel guided them on foot among the rows of big trailing vines with their heart-shaped leaves and their heavy ripe fruit. Eventually he stopped and pointed without speaking. Across a barren patch of soil, a single pumpkin grew by itself, on its own vine, no others within five yards of it.

At first Amanda noticed nothing out of the ordinary; it seemed to be just another Connecticut Field, larger than most, a little darker orange than most. But then she moved closer, and she saw that it was . . . different. She couldn't have said quite how it was different, but there was something . . .

"Well?" Harley said to Manuel. "What about it?"

"You don't feel it, *senor?*"

"No. Feel what?"

But Amanda felt it. She couldn't have explained that either; it was just . . . an aura, a sense of something emanating from the pumpkin that made her uneasy, brought primitive little stirrings of fear and disgust into her mind.

"I do, Harley," she said, and hugged herself. "I know what he means."

"You too? Well, I still say it's nonsense. I'm going to cut it and be done with it. Manuel, let me have your knife . . ."

Manuel backed away, putting his hand over the sharp harvesting knife at his belt. "No, Mr. Sutter. No. You must not!"

"Harley," Amanda said sharply, "he's right. Leave it be."

"Damn. Why should I?"

"It is evil," Manuel said, and looked away from the pumpkin and made the sign of the cross. "It is an evil thing."

"Oh for God's sake. How can a pumpkin be evil?"

Amanda remembered something her uncle, who had been a Presbyterian minister, had said to her when she was a child: *Evil takes many forms, Mandy. Evil shares our bed and eats at our own table. Evil is everywhere, great and small.*

She said, feeling chilled, "Harley, I don't know how, I don't know why, but that pumpkin *is* an evil thing. Leave it alone. Let it rot where it lies."

Manuel crossed himself again. "Yes, *senora!* We will cover it, hide it from the sun, and it will wither and die. It can do no harm if it lies here untouched."

Harley thought they were crazy; that was plain enough. But he let them have their way. He sat in the truck while Manuel went to get a piece of milky plastic rain sheeting and two other men to help him. Amanda stood near the front fender and watched the men cover the pumpkin, anchor the sheeting with wooden stakes and chunks of rock, until they were finished.

Harley had little to say during supper that night, and soon afterward he went out to his workshop in the barn. He was annoyed at what he called her "foolishness," and Amanda couldn't really blame him. The incident with the pumpkin had already taken on a kind of surreal quality in her memory, so that she had begun to think that maybe she and Manuel and the other workers *were* a pack of superstitious fools.

She went out to sit on the porch, bundled up in her heavy wool sweater, as night came down and blacked out the last of the sunset colors over the ocean. An evil pumpkin, she thought. Good Lord, it was ridiculous—a Halloween joke, a sly fantasy tale for children like those that her father used to tell of ghosts and goblins, witches and warlocks, things that go bump in the dark Halloween night. How could a pumpkin be evil? Pumpkins were an utterly harmless fruit: you made pies and cookies from them, you carved them into grinning jack-o'-lanterns; they were a symbol of a grand old tradition, a happy children's rite of fall.

And yet . . .

When she concentrated she could picture the way the strange pumpkin had looked, feel again the vague aura of evil that radiated from it. A small shiver passed through her. Why hadn't Harley felt it too? Some people just weren't sensitive to auras and emanations, she supposed that was it. He was too practical, too logical, too much of a skeptic—a true son of Missouri, the "Show Me" state. He simply couldn't understand.

Understand what? she thought then. I don't understand it either. I don't even know what it is that I'm afraid of.

How did the damned thing get there? Where did it come from? What *is* it?

She found herself looking out toward the east field, as if the pumpkin might somehow be pulsing and glowing under its plastic covering, lighting up the night. There was nothing to see but darkness, of course. Silly. Ridiculous. But if it were picked . . . she did not want to think about what might happen if that woody, furrowed stem were cut, that thick dark orange rind cracked open.

The days passed, and October came, and soon most of the crop had been shipped, the balance put away in the storage shed, and Manuel and the other laborers were gone. All that remained in the fields were the dwarfs and the damaged and withered fruit that had been left to decay into natural fertilizer for the spring planting. And the strange pumpkin near the east fence, hidden under its thick plastic shroud.

Amanda was too busy, as always at harvest time, to think much about the pumpkin. But she did go up there twice, once with Harley and once alone. The first time, Harley wanted to take off the sheeting and look at the thing; she wouldn't let him. The second time, alone, she had stood in a cold sea wind and felt again the emanation of evil, the responsive stirrings of terror and disgust. It was as if the pumpkin were trying to exert some telepathic force upon her, as if it were saying, "Cut my stem . . . open me up . . . eat me . . ." She pulled away finally, almost with a sense of having wrenched loose from grasping hands, and drove away determined to do something drastic: take a can of gasoline up there and set fire to the thing, burn it to a cinder, get *rid* of it once and for all.

But she didn't do it. When she got back to the house she had calmed down and her fears again seemed silly, childish. A telepathic pumpkin, for heaven's sake! A telepathic evil pumpkin! She didn't even tell Harley of the incident.

More days passed, most of October fell away like dry leaves, and the weekend before Halloween arrived—the weekend of the Pumpkin Festival. The crowds were thick on both Saturday and Sunday; Amanda, working the traditional Sutter Farm booth, sold dozens of pumpkins, mainly to families with children who wanted them for Halloween jack-o'-lanterns. She enjoyed herself the first

day, but not the second. Harley entered his prize exhibition pumpkin in the annual contest—it had weighed out finally at 248 pounds
—and fully expected to win his long-awaited second blue ribbon.
And didn't. Aaron Douglas, who owned a farm up near Princeton,
won first prize with a 260-pound Connecticut Field giant.

Harley took the loss hard. He wouldn't eat his supper Sunday
night and moped around on Monday and Halloween Tuesday,
spending most of both days at the stand they always set up near
Highway One to catch any last-minute shoppers. There were several this year: everyone, it seemed, wanted a nice fat pumpkin for
Halloween.

All Hallows' Eve.

Amanda stood at the kitchen window, looking out toward the
fields. It was just after five o'clock, with night settling rapidly; a
low wispy fog had come in off the Pacific and was curling around
the outbuildings, hiding most of the land beyond. She could barely
see the barn, where Harley had gone to his workshop. She wished
he would come back, even if he was still broody over the results of
the contest. It was quiet here in the house, a little too quiet to suit
her, and she felt oddly restless.

Behind her on the stove, hard cider flavored with cinnamon
bubbled in a big iron pot. Harley loved hot cider at this time of
year; he'd had three cups before going out and it had flushed his
face, put a faint slur in his voice—he never had been much of a
drinking man. But she didn't mind. Alcohol loosened him up a bit,
stripped away some of his reserve. Usually it made him laugh, too,
but not tonight.

The fog seemed to be thickening; the lights in the barn had been
reduced to smeary yellow blobs on the gray backdrop. A fine night
for Halloween, she thought. And she smiled a wistful smile as a
pang of nostalgia seized her.

Halloween had been a special night when she was a child, a
night of exciting ritual. First, the carving of the jack-o'-lantern—
how she'd loved that! Her father always brought home the biggest,
roundest pumpkin he could find, and they would scoop it out together, and cut out its eyes and nose and jagged gap-toothed grin,
and light the candle inside, and then set it grinning and glowing on
the porch for all the neighbors to see. Then the dressing up in the
costume her mother had made for her: a witch with a blacked-out
front tooth and a tall-crowned hat, an old broom tucked under one
arm; a ghost dressed in a sewn white sheet, her face smeared with

cold cream; a lady pirate in a crimson tunic and an eye patch, carrying a wooden sword covered in tinfoil. Then the trick-or-treating, and the bags full of candy and gum and fruit and popcorn balls and caramel apples, and the harmless pranks like soaping old Mrs. Collier's windows because she never answered her doorbell, or tying bells to the tail of Mr. Dawson's cat. Then the party afterward, with all her friends from school—cake with Halloween icing and pumpkin pie, blindfold games and bobbing for apples, and afterward, with the lights turned out and the curtains open so they could see the jack-o'-lantern grinning and glowing on the porch, the ghost and goblin stories, and the delicious thrill of terror when her father described the fearful things that prowled and hunted on Hallowmas Eve.

Amanda's smile faded as she remembered that part of the ritual. Her father telling her that Halloween had originated among the ancient Druids, who believed that on this night, legions of evil spirits were called forth by the Lord of the Dead. Saying that the only way to ward them off was to light great fires, and even then . . . even then . . . Saying that on All Hallows' Eve, according to the ancient beliefs, evil was at its strongest and most profound.

Evil like that pumpkin out there?

She shuddered involuntarily and tried to peer past the shimmery outlines of the barn. But the east field was invisible now, clamped inside the bony grasp of the fog. That damned pumpkin! she thought. I *should* have taken some gasoline out there and set fire to it. Exorcism by fire.

Then she thought: Come on, Mandy, that's superstitious nonsense, just like Harley says. The pumpkin is just a pumpkin. Nothing is going to happen here tonight.

But it was so quiet . . .

Abruptly she turned from the window, went to the stove, and picked up her spoon; stirred the hot cider. If Harley didn't come back pretty soon, she'd put on her coat and go out to the workshop and fetch him. She just didn't like being here alone, not tonight of all nights.

So *quiet* . . .

The back door burst open.

She had no warning; the door flew inward, the knob thudding into the kitchen wall, and she cried out the instant she saw him standing there. "Harley! For God's sake, you half scared me to death! What's the idea of—"

Then she saw his face. And what he held dripping in his hand.

She screamed.

He came toward her, and she tried to run, and he caught her and threw her to the floor, pinned her there with his weight. His face loomed above her, stained with stringy pulp and seeds, and she knew what the cider and his brooding had led him to do tonight— knew what was about to happen even before the thing that had been Harley opened its goblin's mouth and the words came out in a drooling litany of evil.

"You're next . . . you're next . . . you're next ..."

The handful of dripping rind and pulp mashed against her mouth as she tried again to scream, forcing some of the bitter juice past her lips. She gagged, fought wildly for a few seconds . . . and then stopped struggling, lay still.

She smiled up at him, a wet dark orange smile.

Now there were two of them, the first two—two to sow the seeds for next year's Halloween harvest.

THE MAYOR OF ASSHOLE VALLEY

NOBODY BETTER try to blame me. All of it, everything that happened and is gonna happen, was Ned Verriker's fault, not mine. Him and that damn label he hung around my neck like a noose.

I remember the night he did it like it was yesterday. A Friday, and five of us were drinking and shooting pool in the Buckhorn Tavern. We weren't a regular group, hell no. We all just happened to be there that night. I almost didn't stick around when I came in and saw Verriker. Him and me just never got along. Big mouth, always yelling and bossing people around at Builders' Supply where he works. Holier than thou too. Drunk Friday and Saturday nights, first one in church on Sunday morning. He didn't like the way I ran my construction business and told me so more than once. Like *he* never cut a few corners in his life. A man's got a right to live the best way he can and he don't need anybody else trying to tell him how to do it.

That afternoon I'd finished the repairs on old Mrs. Evans' sun porch, and she'd paid me in cash like I asked her, and I was feeling good. So I thought the hell with Verriker and stayed put in the Buckhorn to celebrate. I'd've run like hell if I'd had any idea what he was gonna do to me.

Other three in the group were Frank Cummings, Tony Lucchesi, and Ernie Stivic. Frank and me always got along, and Lucchesi was all right for a dago, even if he was a lousy barber. I didn't like Stivic much better than Verriker. Fry cook at the Green Valley Cafe, and I asked him once did he know the difference between a hamburger and a polack burger, just kidding around, and he got right in my face and threatened to bust my arm if I said polack again. Two of the same, him and Verriker. Big-mouthed, hard-nosed bastards.

It was about nine o'clock when we started shooting pool. Verriker's idea. When he was half in the bag he thought he was Fast Eddie Felson. I shoot a better stick than the other three, drunk or sober, so it was me Verriker challenged first. I smoked him for five bucks at Eight Ball. Pissed him off. He claimed I moved the cue ball on one of my shots, but none of the others saw it and I told him he was full of crap. I moved it, all right, but I don't see no reason why a man shouldn't have an edge if he can take it. That goes double against a guy like Verriker.

Well, we played and drank and talked the way you do in bars. Pro football, a game I never liked much. Few jokes, none of them too funny. Politics. Verriker and Stivic were bleeding hearts, and wouldn't you just figure on that? Me, I hate the politics and politicians on both sides. Always raising taxes and passing laws that make it harder for a man to live. Always trying to take away his civil rights, like the right to bear arms.

Work was another topic we got into, and I told how I'd phonied up an invoice to make an extra thousand on time and materials off old lady rich-bitch Evans. I didn't see no reason why I shouldn't talk about it, it was a good trick and a good story, and besides I knew it'd piss Verriker off. It did, all right. He said, "Suppose I tell Mrs. Evans what you did." I said, "Suppose I tell your boss you like young boys." He got hot, called me a dirty son of a bitch and said how about we go outside so he could kick my ass. I worked up a laugh, told him I was only kidding about him liking young boys, and said I'd lied about screwing Mrs. Evans even though it was the truth. I'm not a coward, but he had forty pounds on me and I knew I'd get my clock cleaned if I fought him. My mama didn't raise no damn fools.

He said, "You're an asshole, Pete, you know that?" but I could tell he wasn't so hot to fight anymore. So I let it go. That time I did. I didn't want to light his fire again.

We shot a game of Rotation, and then Cummings got off on a story about how a guy almost ran him off the road that afternoon, some suit in a fancy BMW going about twenty-five mph over the speed limit. Cummings drove a mail truck, drove it like an old lady, so it didn't surprise me none he'd near got forced off the road. Twenty-five over the limit's nothing on the good roads we got in Green Valley. I've gone as much as fifty over myself when I was sure there weren't any sheriff's patrols around. But the others were on Cummings' side.

Lucchesi said, "Yeah, you got to watch yourself every minute these days. People driving too fast, talking on cell phones and not paying attention, jumping lights, cutting you off to save one car-length and five seconds of time."

"You got that right," Stivic said. "Seems there're more assholes on the road every day."

"Not just the roads," Cummings said. "Everywhere you go. It's like some sort of disease. An epidemic of assholes."

Everybody laughed but me. I didn't see what was so funny.

Stivic said, "Christ, you don't suppose they're organized, do you? I mean, a union and everything?"

That got some more laughs. So did what Lucchesi said next. "We ought to put up a sign at the city limits. Big bare buns in a circle with a line through it. No Assholes Allowed."

Subject might've been finished then if it hadn't been for Verriker. Big-mouth had to stick his oar in, have the last word at somebody else's expense. Just had to do it.

He said, "I got a better idea. What we ought to do, we ought to round up all the assholes in the state, maybe even the whole country, and stick 'em together someplace out in the middle of nowhere. Valley like this one, say, only bigger. Have armed guards on duty full time, make sure they all stayed put. Call the place Asshole Valley so there wouldn't be any mistake about who lived there."

"I like it," Stivic said. "By God, I do."

I said, "Well, I don't." I should've kept my lip buttoned, but I was half in the bag myself and I couldn't help it. "I think it's a stupid idea, that's what I think."

"Sure you do, Pete," Verriker said, grinning. "I figured you would."

"What's that supposed to mean? "

"Like I said before. You're an asshole."

He said it loud and it brought down the fucking house. Fifteen or twenty other people in there besides us, they were listening by then and they all busted out laughing too. At what Verriker'd said but it was me they were looking at. Me they were laughing at, not him.

I wanted to smash his face in. If I'd had a bottle or something in my hand, I might've done it. But I just stood there with the blood coming into my face and said, "I'm not an asshole," in a voice as loud as his.

"Bet if we took a vote on that, you'd lose."

"I'm not an asshole!"

"So you say. I say you're the biggest one I know, maybe even the biggest one in these parts."

"You shut up, Verriker. You shut up—"

But he didn't shut up. He was on his feet, moving around, grinning all over his face, playing it up to the crowd. He said, "Matter of fact, if we rounded up all the assholes in the state and put 'em in that valley I was talking about, I bet somebody'd nominate you for mayor. And I bet you'd win hands down. Pete Harmon, the first mayor of Asshole Valley."

Brought the house down again. It made me want to puke, the way they all hooted and high-fived and hooted some more. Looking at me the whole time. Laughing at *me*. Made me sick and shaky and so hot I was afraid I'd pop a blood vessel if I didn't get out of there quick.

Must've looked to Verriker and the rest like I was running away, tail between my legs like a kicked dog. I could hear 'em laughing even after I was out the door. All the way home I heard the laughter and Verriker calling me an asshole, hanging that mayor tag on me.

I didn't sleep much that night. Still felt lousy in the morning. But I had work to do, new construction job starting, a good gimmick where I'd buy some cheap-grade lumber that'd pass for high-grade, make myself another couple of grand. So I went out on the job, and the fag that owned the property and the halfwit kid that worked for me was both standing there grinning. The fag said, "Good morning, Your Honor," and the kid laughed right in my face. That was how fast word had got around. I snapped at them to knock that shit off, I didn't think it was funny, and they saw I meant business and left me alone. But all day long I caught the kid hiding a grin and I knew just what he was thinking, I could almost hear it going round and round inside his head like it was going round and round inside mine.

Pete Harmon, mayor of Asshole Valley.

I knew I was in for a bad time for awhile, but I didn't figure on how bad. It was like a wildfire, the way the story spread around town, the valley, maybe the whole damn county. Everybody out there getting their funnybones tickled at my expense. The fat slob at the store where I did my grocery shopping. Harry Logan at Harry's House of Guns, a guy I'd always thought was my friend. Luke Penny at the Shell station. People who'd been in the Buckhorn that night. First thing Tony Lucchesi said to me was, "Well, if it isn't Hizzoner." And Frank Cummings, all smirk and smartass with "You got your political platform worked out yet, Pete? " And two that were as hard to take as the Buckhorn crowd. Darlene, my cow of an ex-wife, so fat now her ass looks like the back end of a bus, standing in front of City Hall where she works and making ha-ha noises with all her chins jiggling. And the black bastard that clerks in Ingram's Hardware, calling me Mr. Harmon and laughing at me behind his midnight face, thinking even a nigger was better than the mayor of Asshole Valley.

I did all I could to avoid Verriker, but he cornered me too. So much shit come out of *his* mouth I didn't listen to it, I just went away quick like I had urgent business somewhere else. But I could hear him laughing the way he had in the Buckhorn, and the sound stayed in my ears like a poison that wouldn't wash out.

All the crap didn't die down and go away after a few days, like I expected it would. It got worse. Everywhere I went, everybody I come in contact with—wise-ass remarks, grins, giggles, stares, pointing fingers. Kids, even. Some snotnose couldn't've been more than ten, yelling to a bunch of his snotnose buddies, "Hey, there's the guy got elected mayor of the assholes."

Goddamn people! Didn't they know how much a name like that could *hurt?* Calling somebody an asshole to his face was bad enough, but saying he was the biggest asshole around, leader of the pack, and laughing at him and never letting him have any peace, that was the worst you could do to anybody. It cut into a man like a knife, carved out chunks of his insides. Made him half crazy.

It got so bad I couldn't stand to go out of the house. I'd hole up except when I was working, and some days I couldn't even make myself drive over to the job site. I fired the halfwit kid because I couldn't take him looking at me all the time, hiding a grin and laughing at me with his eyes. The fag was just as bad. Started ragging on me about needing to have his shed built before winter, telling me I really ought to show up regular until it was finished. Dressing me down with half his mouth, laughing at me out the other half. A goddamn *fag.*

I had plenty of time to think, holed up in my house, nothing to do but drink too much whiskey and stare at the TV. More I thought, the madder I got. I shouldn't have to take this kind of bullshit. What'd I do to deserve it? Nothing. I wasn't what they were all saying I was. No way. I was just a guy trying to get along the best he could, same as everybody else. None of this was my fault.

Verriker. It was all Verriker's doing.

I kept seeing that smug face of his, hearing him say all them things in the Buckhorn, hearing his poison laugh. I saw his face and heard that laugh in my sleep. Christ, I hated him for what he'd done to me. I never hated anybody as much as I hated Ned Fucking Verriker. I was stuffed so full of hate for him I felt ready to explode.

Get rid of some of it, that was what I had to do. Get rid of his poison. Then maybe I could breathe again.

Get rid of Verriker.

Once the idea come into my head, I couldn't've got it out again if I wanted to. And I didn't want to. I never killed anybody before, nothing human, just deer and ducks and old man Henderson's dog that kept barking its fool head off half the night so a man couldn't sleep. I never wanted to kill anybody before. But I had a real hunger to kill Verriker. I imagined him on the ground, blood running out of him, his eyes all wide and starey like a gutshot, jacklit buck—and it made me laugh out loud. My turn to do the laughing, by God. *My* turn.

"Verriker, dead." It even tasted good in my mouth.

I thought about ways to do it. A gun, sure, that was the simplest, and I had plenty to choose from. I like guns, I like the way they feel in my hands. I had revolvers, deer rifles, a regular pump shotgun and a sawed-off, a Bushmaster assault rifle and a Sterling MK-7 semi-automatic pistol that Harry Logan picked up for me. But I couldn't do it that way. If I just went out and shot the bugger, no matter how careful I was, I'd be the number one suspect. Everybody knew how I felt about Verriker, about that label he'd tied around my neck. He turned up shot, or stabbed or beat over the head with a hunk of wood, the cops'd come straight to my door.

Accident. That was the ticket. Make it look like an accident. Accidents can happen to anybody, any time. They couldn't blame me if Verriker had a fatal one.

So I worked out a plan. It was a good one, clever if I do say so myself, not too risky, and it'd fix him even better than a gun or a knife. His wife Alice would get it too but I didn't care about that. She was almost as bad as him, mouthy, with a tongue sharp as a razor. I hit on her a couple of times when we were in high school, before she started going with Verriker. She wouldn't have nothing to do with me. Told me to my face that my breath smelled bad. Bitch. She had it coming same as he did.

They lived out in the valley, north of town. Semirural. Other houses along the main road to their place, but there was another way to get to it, an old logging road that ran through the woods behind their property line. Not much chance of anybody seeing me if I was careful. I picked a weekday and drove out there early afternoon. Wasn't anybody on the old road, but I parked my van off where it wouldn't be spotted if anybody did come along. Walked the rest of the way with my toolkit.

I didn't have to worry about the house being empty. They both worked in town, her in a beauty shop which was a laugh with a horse face like hers. No kids, no live-in relatives. Alice didn't drive so they always rode in together, came home together. They even made it easy for me to get inside by leaving the back door unlocked.

I took my time looking around, figuring out the details. Easy as pie there too. The garage was attached to the house, with a door that led into the kitchen and a wall switch so you could turn on the kitchen light from out there. Be dark by the time they got home, one of 'em was certain to hit the switch. I rigged it first, so it'd be sure to arc, then exposed the wires in the kitchen light fixture for good measure. Then I loosened the gas line connection behind the stove just enough to let the gas bleed out slow. That was all there was to it.

When I got back to the van I drove up to Stafford, fifteen miles north, and bought some two-by-tens at the lumberyard so I'd have an excuse for being there. I ate an early supper at a coffee shop, and for the first time since the Buckhorn, food tasted good again. Afterward I hunted up a bar I'd never been in before, where no-body'd know me and I wouldn't have to put up with any of that mayor crap. I thought I caught one guy looking my way, laughing at me behind his eyes, but he didn't say anything and he left after one drink so it could've been my imagination. I sucked down half a dozen beers, watching the TV they had going on the backbar. That's how I got the word.

News flash. Big explosion in Green Valley, house completely destroyed, both residents killed instantly. Ned and Alice Verriker. Blown to pieces.

I paid my tab and went out to the van and laughed so hard I couldn't drive for ten minutes.

That night I slept straight through, no dreams of Verriker or anybody else laughing or calling me names. In the morning I felt fine, in the pink. Most of the big hate was gone. Verriker's poison too. I figured now I could go out and start living my old life again.

Wrong. Dead wrong.

It was the same as before, only worse.

All anybody wanted to talk about was the explosion. None of 'em thought it was anything but an accident—neither did the law, sheriff never hassled me at all—but that didn't stop them from yacking about it. Verriker this and Verriker that. Poor Ned and poor Alice. I ran into Frank Cummings just pulling his mail truck out of the post office lot, and he looked at me like I was a pile of dog turds. "You're one person's not sorry about Ned, huh, Mr. Mayor?" he said.

He was the first with the mayor crap but he wasn't the last. That day, all that week, I heard it from Stivic, Luke Penny, half the goddamn town. Looking at me the way Cummings had, wrinkling their noses like they couldn't stand my smell. Laughing at me with their eyes. Pulling the noose so tight I couldn't breathe.

I started to hear the laughter and the voices in my sleep again. And Verriker's was the loudest. *Biggest one I know, maybe the biggest one in these parts. I bet somebody'd nominate you for mayor, I bet you'd win hands down. Pete Harmon, the first mayor of Asshole Valley . . . mayor of Asshole Valley . . . mayor of Asshole Valley.*

The poison was back. And so was my hate, bigger and hotter than before. Killing Verriker hadn't done a damn bit of good. The noose was tied too tight, the poison in too deep. I couldn't live like a normal man anymore. Couldn't get rid of those laughing voices awake or asleep—they just kept playing over and over like they were on some kind of loop inside my head.

Whiskey didn't help, no matter how much I drank. Except for one night. That night it made everything clear instead of murky, like booze does sometimes, and I saw what I should've seen a lot sooner. I saw it clear as looking through a pane of new glass.

Verriker and Stivic and Lucchesi and Darlene and Penny and all the rest of 'em were the real assholes. Green Valley wasn't Green Valley anymore—it was Asshole Valley.

I knew I had to do something about that. Maybe their poison ran too deep in me to get flushed out, but it wasn't too late to stop it from spreading, poisoning everybody outside Asshole Valley. But what could I do? Chrissake, I couldn't kill them all like I'd killed Verriker and his old lady. Not one or two at a time, I couldn't.

No, not one or two at a time.

It come to me just like that, what I had to do. Seemed crazy at first, but the more I thought about it the saner it got. Wasn't even revenge, when you looked at it the right way. It was justice. What they call redressing a wrong.

This was Asshole Valley now, and if the assholes thought of me as the mayor, all right, I'd take the job temporarily. I'd be the kind of mayor ran his town with an iron fist and showed no mercy, a Mayor with a capital M. I'd clean out the assholes once and for all. Make the valley Green again.

Once I saw things like that, I couldn't wait to do the job. Sooner it got done, sooner I'd have the last laugh.

So I made my plans. And started stockpiling what I'd need. Dynamite was the first thing I thought of because it'd be easy to get. Anybody with a construction license can buy as many sticks as he wants, hardly any questions asked. But dynamite can be unreliable and I'd have to pack in a hell of a lot to do the job right. C-4 plastic explosive, the kind they used in 'Nam, was more compact, more powerful. I'd never used it but I'd read about it in *Soldier of Fortune.* Harry Logan put me in touch with a guy downstate he said would sell me anything I wanted for the right price. I didn't tell Harry why I was interested in hooking up with that kind of supplier and he didn't ask. That's the good thing about Harry, he knows how to keep his mouth shut. One of the few didn't throw crap in my face except for that one time. He's not one of the assholes.

I took some of the tax-free cash I'd salted away in my safe deposit box and drove down south and bought all the C-4 I'd need. Timers and some other stuff too. The guy had a hell of a selection, everything from flak jackets to hollow-point ammo to mortars and grenade launchers.

When I got back to Asshole Valley I went right to work planting the charges with timers hooked up to 'em. The Buckhorn Tavern was easy—took me less than an hour to get in and out after they closed up one night. City Hall was harder. I had to hide four charges there, to make sure the whole thing would come down, and getting inside without being spotted wasn't easy. Took me two nights and I had a couple of close calls, but I managed it. Damn right I did. I even tucked a little ball of C-4 into the air-conditioning duct in the mayor's office for good measure, and you better believe I had a good laugh about that when I got home.

I had the timers set for the same day, a few hours apart. City Hall first, mid-afternoon, and the Buckhorn at six o'clock when it was sure to be packed full of assholes talking about the City Hall blowup. Five days to wait, when I was all done. Then the fun would start. Goodbye, assholes.

Yesterday, four days until Boom Time, I had *another* brain-storm. Why stop with Asshole Valley? The assholes here aren't the only ones around by a long shot. Plenty of big ones that deserve the same as this bunch is gonna get. Big fish for the Mayor to fry. I got plenty of C-4 and timers left over. I got my Bushmaster assault rifle and MK-7 pistol, and some hollow-point ammo, and a case of fragmentation grenades and a launcher I picked up down south. Everything I'll need no matter which other targets I decide on when I get to where I'm going.

Too bad I won't be able to watch the fun here after all. But I got to get moving while there's still enough time. My van's all loaded and ready to roll.

Look out, you assholes in Washington, here comes the Mayor!

CHIP

JOHN VALARIAN felt as he always did when he came to St. Ives Academy—a little awkward and uncomfortable, as if he didn't really belong in a place like this. St. Ives was one of the most exclusive, expensive boys' schools on the east coast, but that wasn't the reason; he'd picked it out himself, over Andrea's objections, when Peter reached his eighth birthday two years ago. The wooded country setting and hundred-year-old stone buildings weren't the reason, either. It was what the school represented, the atmosphere you felt as soon as you entered the grounds. Knowledge. Good breeding. Status. Class.

Well, maybe he *didn't* belong here. He'd come out of the city slums, had to fight for every rung on his way up the ladder. He hadn't had much schooling, still had trouble reading. And he'd never been able to polish off all his rough edges. That was one of the reasons he was determined to give his son the best education money could buy.

He climbed the worn stone steps of the administration building, gave his name to the lobby receptionist. She directed him up another flight of stairs to the headmaster's office. He'd been there once before, on the day he'd brought Peter here for enrollment, but he didn't remember much about it except that he'd been deeply impressed. This was only his third visit to St. Ives in three years—just two short ones before today. It made him feel bad, neglectful, thinking about it now. He'd intended to come more often, particularly for the father-son days, but some business matter always got in the way. Business ruled him. He didn't like it sometimes, but that was the way it was. Some things you couldn't change no matter what.

The headmaster kept him waiting less than five minutes. His name was Locklear. Late fifties, silver-haired, looked exactly like you'd expect the head of St. Ives Academy to look. When they were alone in his private office, Locklear shook hands gravely and said, "Thank you for coming, Mr. Valarian. Please sit down."

He perched on the edge of a maroon leather chair, now tense and on guard as well as uncomfortable. The way he'd felt when he got sent to the principal's office in public school. He didn't know what to do with his hands, finally slid them down tight over his knees. His gaze roamed the office. Nice. Books everywhere, a big illuminated globe on a wooden stand, a desk that had to be pure Philippine mahogany, a bank of windows that looked out over the central quadrangle and rolling lawns beyond. Impressive, all right. He wouldn't mind having a desk like that one himself.

He waited until Locklear was seated behind it before he said, "This trouble with my son. It must be pretty serious if you couldn't talk about it on the phone."

"I'm afraid it is. Quite serious."

"Bad grades or what?"

"No. Chip is extremely bright, and his grades—"

"Peter."

"Ah, yes, of course."

"His mother calls him Chip. I don't."

"He seems to prefer it."

"His name is Peter. Chip sounds . . . ordinary."

"Your son is anything but ordinary, Mr. Valarian."

The way the headmaster said that tightened him up even more. "What's going on here?" he demanded. "What's Peter done?"

"We're not absolutely certain he's responsible for any of the . . . incidents. I should make that clear at the outset. However, the circumstantial evidence is considerable and points to no one else."

Incidents. Circumstantial evidence. "Get to the point, Mr. Locklear. What do you *think* he did?"

The headmaster leaned forward, made a steeple of his fingertips. He seemed to be hiding behind it as he said, "There have been a series of thefts in Chip's . . . in Peter's dormitory, beginning several weeks ago. Small amounts of cash taken from the rooms of nearly a dozen different boys."

"My son's not a thief."

"I sincerely hope that's so. But as I said, the circumstantial evidence—"

"Why would he steal money? He's got plenty of his own—I send him more than he can spend every month."

"I can't answer your question. I wish I could."

"You ask him about the thefts?"

"Yes."

"And?"

"He denies taking any money."

"All right then," Valarian said. "If he says he didn't do it, then he didn't do it."

"Two of the victims saw him coming out of their rooms immediately before they discovered missing sums."

"And you believe these kids over my son."

"Given the other circumstances, we have no choice."

"What other circumstances?"

"Chip has been involved in—"

"Peter."

"I'm sorry, yes, Peter. He has been involved in several physical altercations recently. Last week one of the boys he attacked suffered a broken nose."

"Attacked? How do you know he did the attacking?"

"There were witnesses," Locklear said. "To that assault and to the others. In each case, they swore Peter was the aggressor."

The office seemed to have grown too warm; Valarian could feel himself starting to sweat. "He's a little aggressive, I admit that. Always has been. A lot of kids his age—"

"His behavior goes beyond simple aggression, I'm afraid. I can only describe it as bullying to the point of terrorizing."

"Come on, now. I don't believe that."

"Nevertheless, it's true. If you'd care to talk to his teachers, his classmates . . ."

Valarian shook his head. After a time he said, "If this has been going on for a while, why didn't you let me know before?"

"At first the incidents were isolated, and without proof that Peter was responsible for the thefts . . . well, we try to give our young men the benefit of the doubt whenever possible. But as they grew more frequent, more violent, I *did* inform you of the problem. Twice by letter, once in a message when I couldn't reach you by phone at your office."

He stared at the headmaster, but it was only a few seconds before his disbelief faded and he lowered his gaze. Two letters, one phone call. Dimly he remembered getting one of the letters, reading it, dismissing it as unimportant because he was in the middle of a big transaction with the Chicago office. The other letter . . . misplaced, inadvertently thrown out or filed. The phone call . . . dozens came in every day, he had two secretaries screening them and taking messages, and sometimes the messages didn't get delivered.

He didn't know what to say. He sat there sweating, feeling like a fool.

"Last evening there was another occurrence," Locklear said, "the most serious of all. That is why I called this morning and insisted on speaking to you in person. We can't prove that your son is responsible, but given what we do know we can hardly come to another conclusion."

"What occurrence? What happened last night?"

"Someone," Locklear said carefully, "set fire to our gymnasium."

"Set fire— My God."

"Fortunately it was discovered in time to prevent it from burning out of control and destroying the entire facility, but it did cause several thousand dollars' damage."

"What makes you think Peter set it?"

"He had an argument with his physical education instructor yesterday afternoon. He became quite abusive and made thinly veiled threats. It was in the instructor's office that kerosene was poured and the fire set."

Valarian opened his mouth, clicked it shut again. He couldn't seem to think clearly now. Too damn quiet in there; he could hear a clock ticking somewhere. He broke the silence in a voice that sounded like a stranger's.

"What're you going to do? Expel him? Is that why you got me up here?"

"Believe me, Mr. Valarian, it pains me to say this, but yes, that is the board's decision. For the welfare of St. Ives Academy and the other students. Surely you can understand."

"Oh, I understand," Valarian said bitterly "You bet I understand."

"Peter will be permitted to remain here until the end of the week, under supervision, if you require time to make other arrangements for him. Of course, if you'd rather he leave with you this afternoon . . ."

Valarian got jerkily to his feet. "I want to talk to my son. Now."

"Yes, naturally. I sent for him earlier and he's waiting in one of the rooms just down the hall."

He had to fight his anger as he followed the headmaster to where Peter was waiting. He felt like hitting something or somebody. Not the boy, he'd never laid a hand on him and never would. Not Locklear, either. Somebody. Himself, maybe.

Locklear stopped before a closed door. He said somberly, "I'll await you in my office, Mr. Valarian," and left him there alone.

He hesitated before going in, to calm down and work out how he was going to handle this. All right. He took a couple of heavy breaths and opened the door.

The boy was sitting on a straightback chair—not doing anything, just sitting there like a statue. When he saw his father he got slowly to his feet and stood with his arms down at his sides. No smile, nothing but a blank stare. He looked older than ten. Big for his age, lean but wide through the shoulders. *He looks like I did at that age,* Valarian thought. *He looks just like me.*

"Hello, Peter."

"Chip," the boy said in a voice as blank as his stare. "You know I prefer Chip, Papa."

"Your name is Peter. I prefer Peter."

Valarian crossed the room to him. The boy put out his hand, but on impulse Valarian bent and caught his shoulders and hugged him. It was like hugging a piece of stone. Valarian let go of him, stepped back.

"I just had a long talk with your headmaster," he said. "Those thefts, the fire yesterday . . . he says it was you."

"I know."

"Well? Was it?"

"No, Papa."

"Don't lie to me. If you did all that . . ."

"I didn't. I didn't do anything."

"They're kicking you out of St. Ives. They wouldn't do that if they weren't sure it was you."

"I don't care."

"You don't care you're being expelled?"

"I don't like it here anymore. I don't care what the headmaster or the teachers or the other kids think. I don't care what anybody thinks about me." Funny little smile. "Except you, Papa."

"All right," Valarian said. "Look me in the eyes and tell me the truth. *Did* you steal money, set that fire?"

"I already told you I didn't."

"In my eyes. Up close."

The boy stepped forward and looked at him squarely. "No, Papa, I didn't," he said.

In the car on the way back to the city he kept seeing Peter's eyes staring into his. He couldn't get them out of his mind. What he'd seen there shining deep and dark ... it must've been there all along. How could he have missed it before? It had made him feel cold all over; made him want nothing more to do with his son to-day, tell Locklear he'd send somebody to pick up the boy at the end of the week and then get out of there fast. Now, remembering, it made him shudder.

Lugo was looking at him in the rear view mirror. "Something wrong, Mr. Valarian?"

At any other time he'd have said no and let it go at that. But now he heard himself say, "It's my son. He got into some trouble. That's why I had to go to the school."

"All taken care of now?"

"No. They're throwing him out."

"No kidding? That's too bad."

"Is it?" Then he said, "His name's Peter, but his mother calls him Chip. She says he's like me, a chip off the same block. He likes the name, he thinks it fits him too. But I don't like it."

"How come?"

"I don't want him to be like me, I wanted him to grow up better than me. Better in every way. That's why I sent him to St. Ives. You understand?"

Lugo said, "Yes, sir," but they were just words. Lugo was his driver, his bodyguard, his strongarm man; all Lugo understood was how to steer a limo, how to serve the mob with muscle or a gun.

"I don't want him in my business," Valarian said. "I don't want him to be another John Valarian."

"But now you think maybe he will be?"

"No, that's not what I think." Valarian crossed himself, pictur-ing those bright, cold eyes. "I think he's gonna be a hell of a lot worse."

THE WINNING TICKET

A "Nameless Detective" Story

J AKE RUNYON and I were hunched over mugs of coffee and tea in an all-night diner near the Cow Palace when the man and woman blew in out of the rain.

Blew in is the right phrase. They came fast through the door, leaning forward, prodded by the howling wind. Nasty night out there. One of the hard-rain, big-wind storms that sometimes hammer the California coast during an El Nino winter.

The man shook himself doglike, shedding rainwater off a shaved head and a threadbare topcoat, before the two of them slid into one of the side-wall booths. That was as much attention as I paid to them at first. He wasn't the man we were waiting for.

"After eleven," I said to Runyon. "Looks like Maxwell's a no-show again tonight."

"Weather like this, he'll probably stay holed up."

"And so we get to do it all over again tomorrow night."

"You want to give it a few more minutes?"

"Might as well. At least until the rain lets up a little."

Floyd Maxwell was a deadbeat dad, the worst kind. Spousal abuser who owed his ex more than thirty thousand dollars in unpaid child support for their two kids; hard to catch because he kept moving around in and out of the city, never staying in one place longer than a couple of months, and because he had the kind of job—small-business computer consultant—that allowed him to work from any location. Our agency had been hired by the ex's father and we'd tracked Maxwell to this neighborhood, but we'd been unable to pinpoint an exact address; all we knew was that since he'd moved here, he ate in the Twenty-Four Seven Diner most evenings after ten o'clock, when there were few customers. Bracing him was a two-man job because of his size and his history of violent behavior. Runyon was twenty years younger than me, a former Seattle cop with a working knowledge of judo; Tamara and I couldn't have hired a tougher or more experienced field operative when we'd decided to expand the agency.

This was our third night staked out here and so far all we had to show for it were sour stomachs from too much caffeine. I had mixed feelings about the job anyway. On the one hand I don't like deadbeat dads or spousal abusers and nailing one is always a source of satisfaction. On the other hand it amounted to a bounty hunt, the two of us sitting here with handcuffs in our pockets waiting to make a citizens' arrest of a fugitive, and I've never much cared for that kind of strongarm work. Or the type of people who do it for a living.

The new couple were the only other customers right now. The counterman, a thin young guy with a long neck and not much chin, leaned over the counter and called out to them, "What can I get you folks?"

"Coffee," the man said. He was about forty, well set up, pasty-faced and hard-eyed. Some kind of tattoo crawled up the side of his neck; another covered the back of one hand. He glanced at the woman. "You want anything, Lila?"

"No."

"Couple of hamburgers to go," he said to the counterman. "One with everything, one with just the meat. Side of fries."

"Anything to drink with that?"

"More coffee, biggest you got. Milk."

"For the coffee?"

"In a carton. For drinking."

The counterman said, "Coming up," and turned to the grill.

The tattooed guy said to the woman, "You better have something. We got a long drive ahead of us."

"I couldn't eat, Kyle." She was maybe thirty, a washed-out, purse-lipped blond who might have been pretty once—the type who perpetually make the wrong choices with the wrong people and show the effects. "I feel kind of sick."

"Yeah? Why didn't you stay in the car?"

"You know why. I couldn't listen to it any more."

"Well, you better get used to it."

"It breaks my heart. I still think—"

"I don't care what you think. Just shut up."

Lila subsided, slouching down in the booth so that her head rested against the low back. Runyon and I were both watching them now, without being obvious about it. Eye-corner studies with our heads held still.

Pretty soon the woman said, "Why'd we have to stop here, so close? Why couldn't we just keep going?"

"It's a lousy night and I'm hungry."

"Hungry. After what just happened I don't see how you—"

"Didn't I just tell you to shut up?"

The counterman set a mug of steaming coffee on the counter. "You'll have to come get it," he said. "I got to watch the burgers."

Neither of the pair made a move to leave the booth. Kyle leaned forward and snapped at her in a low voice, "Well? Don't just sit there like a dummy. Get the coffee."

Grimacing, she slid out and fetched the coffee for him. She didn't sit down again. "I don't feel so good," she said.

"So go outside, get some air."

"No. I think I'm gonna be sick."

"Yeah, well, don't do it here."

She turned away from him, putting a hand up to cover her mouth, and half-ran into the areaway that led to the rest rooms. A door slammed back there. Kyle loaded sugar into his coffee, made slurping sounds as he drank it.

"Hurry up with the food," he called to the counterman.

"Almost ready."

It got quiet in there, except for the meat-sizzle on the grill, the French fries cooking in their basket of hot oil. Outside, the wind continued to beat at the front of the diner, but the rain seemed to have slacked off some.

Runyon and I watched Kyle finish his coffee. For a few seconds he sat drumming on the tabletop. Then he smacked it with his palm, slid out, and came up to the counter two stools down from where we were sitting. He stood watching the counterman wrap the burgers in waxed paper, put them into a sack with the fries; pour coffee into one container, milk into another.

"How much?" he said.

"Just a second while I ring it up."

Kyle looked over toward the areaway, scowling. Lila still hadn't reappeared.

"Hope your friend's okay," the counterman said.

"Just mind your own business, pal."

The total for the food was twelve dollars. Kyle dragged a worn wallet out of his pocket, slapped three bills down next to the two bags. When he did that I had a clear look at the tattoo on his wrist—Odin's Cross. There were bloody scrapes across the knuckles on that hand, crimson spots on the sleeve of his topcoat; the blood hadn't completely coagulated yet. Under the open coat, on the left side at the belt, I had a glimpse of wood and metal.

I was closest to him and he caught me paying attention. "What the hell you looking at?"

I didn't say anything.

"Keep your eyes to yourself, you know what's good for you."

I let that pass too.

Lila came out of the rest room looking pale. "About the damn time," Kyle said to her.

"I couldn't help it. I told you I was sick."

"Take those sacks and let's go."

She picked up the sacks and they started for the door. As far as Lila was concerned, the rest of us weren't even there; she was focused on Kyle and her own misery. Otherwise she might've been more careful about what she said on the way.

"Kyle . . .you won't hurt him, will you?"

"Don't be stupid."

"You hit him twice already . . ."

"A couple of slaps, big deal. He's not hurt."

"You get crazy sometimes. What you did to his mother—"

"Dammit, keep your voice down."

"But what if she calls the—"

"She won't. She knows better. Now shut up!"

They were at the door by then. And out into the gibbering night.

I glanced at Runyon. "Who's the plain burger and milk for, if she's too sick to eat?"

"Yeah," he said, and we were both off our stools and moving. Trust your instincts.

At the door I said, "Watch yourself. He's armed."

"I know, I saw it too."

Outside the rain had eased up to a fine drizzle, but the wind was still beating the night in bone-chilling gusts. The slick black street and sidewalks were empty except for the two of them off to our right, their backs to us, Kyle moving around to the driver's door of a Suburu Outback parked two car-lengths away. There was a beeping sound as he used the remote on his key chain to unlock the doors.

Runyon and I made our approach in long silent strides, not too fast. You don't want to run or make noise in a situation like this; it only invites a panic reaction. What we did once Kyle saw us depended on what he did. The one thing we wouldn't do was to give chase if he jumped into the car, locked the doors, and drove away; that kind of nonsense is strictly Hollywood. In that scenario we'd back off and call it in and let the police handle it.

The woman, Lila, opened the passenger side door. The dome light came on, providing a vague lumpish view of a rear cargo space packed with suitcases and the like. But it was what spilled out from inside, identifiable in the wind-lull that followed, that tightened muscles all through my body. A child crying—broken, frightened sobs that went on and on.

We were nearing the Outback by then, off the curb and into the street. Close enough to make out the rain-spattered license plate. 5QQX700—an easy one to remember. But I didn't need to remember it. The way things went down, the plate number was irrelevent.

Lila saw us first. She called, "Kyle!" and jerked back from the open passenger door.

He was just opening the driver's side. He came around fast, but he didn't do anything else for a handful of seconds. Just stood there staring at us as we advanced, still at the measured pace, Runyon a couple of steps to my left so we both had a clear path to him.

Runyon put up a hand, making it look nonthreatening, and said in neutral tones, "Talk to you for a minute?"

No. It wasn't going to go down that way—reasonable, nonviolent.

At just that moment a car swung around the corner up ahead, throwing mist-smeared headlight glare over the four of us and the Outback. The light seemed to jump-start Kyle. He didn't try to get inside; he jammed the door shut and went for the weapon he had under his coat.

Runyon got to him first, just as the gun came out, and knocked his arm back.

A beat or two later I shoulldered into him, hard, pinning the left side of his body against the wet metal. That gave Runyon time to judo-chop his wrist and loosen his grip on the gun. A second chop drove it right out of his hand, sent it clattering along the pavement.

Things got a little wild then. Kyle fought us, snarling; he was big and angry and even though there were two of us, just as big, he was no easy handful. The woman stood off from the Outback, yelling like a banshee. The other car, the one with the lights, skidded to a stop across the street. The wind howled, the child shrieked. I had a vague aural impression of running footsteps, someone else yelling.

It took maybe a minute's worth of teamwork to put an end to the struggle. I managed finally to get a two-handed hold on Kyle's arms, which allowed Runyon to step free and slam the edge of his hand down on the exposed joining of neck and shoulder. The blow paralyzed the right side of Kyle's body. After that we were able to wrestle him to the wet pavement, stretch him out belly down. I pulled his arms back and held them while Runyon knelt in the middle of his back, snapped handcuffs around his wrists.

I stood up first, breathing hard—and a white, scared face was peering at me through the rear side window. A little boy, six or seven, wrapped in a blanket, his cheeks streaked with tears. Past him, on the other side of the car, I could see Lila standing, quiet now, with both hands fisted against her mouth.

Runyon said, "Where's the gun?"

"I don't know. I heard it hit the pavement—"

"I've got it."

I turned around. It was the guy from the car that had pulled up across the street; he'd come running over to rubberneck. He stood a short distance away, holding the revolver in one hand, loosely, as if he didn't know what to do with it. Heavy-set and bald, I saw as I went up to him. Eyebrows like miniature tumbleweeds.

"What's going on?" he said.

"Police business."

"Yeah? You guys cops?"

"Making an arrest." I held out my hand, palm up. "Let's have the gun."

He hesitated, but just briefly. Then he said, "Sure, sure," and laid it on my palm.

And I backed up a step and pointed it at a spot two inches below his chin.

"Hey!" He gawped at me in disbelief. "Hey, what's the idea?"

"The idea," I said, "is for you to turn around, slow, and clasp your hands together behind you. Do it—now!"

He did it. He didn't have any choice.

I gave the weapon to Runyon. And then, shaking my head, smiling a little, I snapped my set of handcuffs around Floyd Maxwell's wrists.

Funny business, detective work. Crazy business sometimes. Mostly it's a lot of dull routine, with small triumphs and as much frustration as satisfaction. But once in a great while something happens that not only makes it all worthwhile but defies the laws of probability. Call it whatever you like—random accident, multiple coincidence, star-and-planet convergence, fate, blind luck, divine intervention. It happens. It happened to Jake Runyon and me that stormy February night.

An ex-con named Kyle Franklin, fresh out of San Quentin after serving six years for armed robbery, decides he wants sole custody of his seven-year-old son. He drags his girlfriend to San Francisco, where his former wife is raising the boy as a single mom, and beats and threatens the ex-wife and kidnaps the child. Rather than leave the city quick, he decides he needs some sustenance for the long drive to Lila's place in L.A. and stops at the first diner he sees, less than a quarter mile from the ex-wife's apartment building—a diner where two case-hardened private detectives happen to be staked out.

We overhear part of his conversation with Lisa and it sounds wrong to us. We notice the blood on his coat sleeve, the scraped knuckles, his prison pallor, the Odin's Cross—a prison tattoo and racist symbol—on his wrist, and the fact that he's carrying a concealed weapon. So we follow him outside and brace him, he pulls the gun, and while we're struggling, our deadbeat dad chooses that moment to show up. The smart thing for Maxwell to have done was to drive off, avoid trouble; instead he lets his curiosity and arrogance get the best of him, and comes over to watch, and then picks up Franklin's gun and hands it to me nice as you please. And so we foil a kidnapping and put the arm on not one but two violent, abusive fathers in the space of about three minutes.

What are the odds? Astronomical. You could live three or four lifetimes and nothing like it would ever happen again.

It's a little like hitting the megabucks state lottery.

That night, Runyon and I were the ones holding the winning ticket.

PEEKABOO

ROPER CAME AWAKE with the feeling that he wasn't alone in the house.

He sat up in bed, tense and wary, a crawling sensation on the back of his scalp. The night was dark, moonless; warm clotted black surrounded him. He rubbed sleep mucus from his eyes, blinking, until he could make out the vague grayish outlines of the open window in one wall, the curtains fluttering in the hot summer breeze.

Ears straining, he listened. But there wasn't anything to hear. The house seemed almost graveyard-still, void of even the faintest of night sounds.

What was it that had woken him up? A noise of some kind? An intuition of danger? It might only have been a bad dream, except that he couldn't remember dreaming. And it might only have been imagination, except that the feeling of not being alone was strong, urgent.

There's somebody in the house, he thought.

Or some *thing* in the house?

In spite of himself Roper remembered the story the nervous real estate agent in Whitehall had told him about this place. It had been built in the early 1900s by a local family, and when the last of them died off a generation later it was sold to a man named Lavolle who had lived in it for forty years. Lavolle had been a recluse whom the locals considered strange and probably evil; they hadn't had anything to do with him. But then he'd died five years ago, of natural causes, and evidence had been found by county officials that he'd been "some kind of devil worshiper" who had "practiced all sorts of dark rites." That was all the real estate agent would say about it.

Word had got out and a lot of people seemed to believe the house was haunted or cursed or something. For that reason, and because it was isolated and in ramshackle condition, it had stayed empty until a couple of years ago. Then a man called Garber, who was an amateur parapsychologist, leased the place and lived here for ten days. At the end of that time somebody came out from

Whitehall to deliver groceries and found Garber dead. Murdered.
The real estate agent wouldn't talk about how he'd been killed;
nobody else would talk about it either.

Some people thought it was ghosts or demons that had murdered Garber. Others figured it was a lunatic—maybe the same
one who'd killed half a dozen people in this part of New England
over the past couple of years. Roper didn't believe in ghosts or
demons or things that went bump in the night; that kind of supernatural stuff was for rural types like the ones in Whitehall. He believed in psychotic killers, all right, but he wasn't afraid of them;
he wasn't afraid of anybody or anything. He'd made his living
with a gun too long for that. And the way things were for him
now, since the bank job in Boston had gone sour two weeks ago,
an isolated backcountry place like this was just what he needed for
a few months.

So he'd leased the house under a fake name, claiming to be a
writer, and he'd been here for eight days. Nothing had happened in
that time: no ghosts, no demons, no strange lights or wailings or
rattling chains—and no lunatics or burglars or visitors of any kind.
Nothing at all.

Until now.

Well, if he *wasn't* alone in the house, it was because somebody
human had come in. And he sure as hell knew how to deal with a
human intruder. He pushed the blankets aside, swung his feet out
of bed, and eased open the nightstand drawer. His fingers groped
inside, found his .38 revolver and the flashlight he kept in there
with it; he took them out. Then he made his way carefully across
to the bedroom door, opened it a crack to listen again.

The same heavy silence.

Roper pulled the door wide, switched on the flash, and probed
the hallway with its beam. No one there. He stepped out, moving
on the balls of his bare feet. There were four other doors along the
hallway: two more bedrooms, a bathroom, and an upstairs sitting
room. He opened each of the doors in turn, swept the rooms with
the flash, then put on the overhead lights.

Empty, all of them.

He came back to the stairs. Shadows clung to them, filled the
wide foyer below. He aimed the light down there from the landing.
Bare mahogany walls, the lumpish shapes of furniture, more shadows crouching inside the arched entrances to the parlor and the
library. But that was all: no sign of anybody, still no sounds anywhere in the warm dark.

He went down the stairs, swinging the light from side to side. At the bottom he stopped next to the newel post and used the beam to slice into the blackness in the center hall. Deserted. He arced it around into the parlor, followed it with his body turned sideways to within a pace of the archway. More furniture, the big fieldstone fireplace at the far wall, the parlor windows reflecting glints of light from the flash. He glanced back at the heavy darkness inside the library, didn't see or hear any movement over that way, and reached out with his gun hand to flick the switch on the wall inside the parlor.

Nothing happened when the electric bulbs in the old-fashioned chandelier came on; there wasn't anybody in there.

Roper crossed to the library arch and scanned the interior with the flash. Empty bookshelves, empty furniture. He put on the chandelier. Empty room.

He swung the cone of light past the staircase, into the center hall—and then brought it back to the stairs and held it there. The area beneath them had been walled on both sides, as it was in a lot of these old houses, to form a coat or storage closet; he'd found that out when he first moved in and opened the small door that was set into the staircase on this side. But it was just an empty space now, full of dust—

The back of his scalp tingled again. And a phrase from when he was a kid playing hide-and-seek games popped into his mind.

Peekaboo, I see you. Hiding under the stair.

His finger tightened around the butt of the .38. He padded forward cautiously, stopped in front of the door. And reached out with the hand holding the flash, turned the knob, jerked the door open, and aimed the light and the gun inside.

Nothing.

Roper let out a breath, backed away to where he could look down the hall again. The house was still graveyard-quiet; he couldn't even hear the faint grumblings its old wooden joints usually made in the night. It was as if the whole place was wrapped in a breathless waiting hush. As if there was some kind of unnatural presence at work here—

Screw that, he told himself angrily. No such things as ghosts and demons. There seemed to be a presence here, all right—he could feel it just as strongly as before—but it was a human presence. Maybe a burglar, maybe a tramp, maybe even a goddamn lunatic. But *human*.

He snapped on the hall lights and went along there to the arch-way that led into the downstairs sitting room. First the flash and then the electric wall lamps told him it was deserted. The dining room off the parlor next. And the kitchen. And the rear porch.

Still nothing.

Where was he, damn it? Where was he hiding?

The cellar? Roper thought.

It didn't make sense that whoever it was would have gone down there. The cellar was a huge room, walled and floored in stone, that ran under most of the house; there wasn't anything in it except spiderwebs and stains on the floor that he didn't like to think about, not after the real estate agent's story about Lavolle and his dark rites. But it was the only place left that he hadn't searched.

In the kitchen again, Roper crossed to the cellar door. The knob turned soundlessly under his hand. With the door open a crack, he peered into the thick darkness below and listened. Still the same heavy silence.

He started to reach inside for the light switch. But then he re-membered that there wasn't any bulb in the socket above the stairs; he'd explored the cellar by flashlight before, and he hadn't bothered to buy a bulb. He widened the opening and pointed the flash downward, fanning it slowly from left to right and up and down over the stone walls and floor. Shadowy shapes appeared and disappeared in the bobbing light: furnace, storage shelves, a wooden wine rack, the blackish gleaming stains at the far end, spi-derwebs like tattered curtains hanging from the ceiling beams.

Roper hesitated. Nobody down there either, he thought. No-body in the house after all? The feeling that he wasn't alone kept nagging at him—but it *could* be nothing more than imagination. All that business about devil-worshiping and ghosts and demons and Garber being murdered and psychotic killers on the loose might have affected him more than he'd figured. Might have jum-bled together in his subconscious all week and finally come out tonight, making him imagine menace where there wasn't any. Sure, maybe that was it.

But he had to make certain. He couldn't see all of the cellar, from up here; he had to go down and give it a full search before he'd be satisfied that he really was alone. Otherwise he'd never be able to get back to sleep tonight.

Playing the light again, he descended the stairs in the same wary movements as before. The beam showed him nothing. Except for the faint whisper of his breathing, the creak of the risers when he put his weight on them, the stillness remained unbroken. The odors of dust and decaying wood and subterranean dampness dilated his nostrils; he began to breathe through his mouth.

When he came off the last of the steps he took a half dozen strides into the middle of the cellar. The stones were cold and clammy against the soles of his bare feet. He turned to his right, then let the beam and his body transcribe a slow circle until he was facing the stairs.

Nothing to see, nothing to hear.

But with the light on the staircase, he realized that part of the wide, dusty area beneath them was invisible from where he stood—a mass of clotted shadow. The vertical boards between the risers kept the beam from reaching all the way under there.

The phrase from when he was a kid repeated itself in his mind: *Peekaboo, I see you. Hiding under the stair.*

With the gun and the flash extended at arm's length, he went diagonally to his right. The light cut away some of the thick gloom under the staircase, letting him see naked stone draped with more gray webs. He moved closer to the stairs, ducked under them, and put the beam full on the far joining of the walls.

Empty.

For the first time Roper began to relax. Imagination, no doubt about it now. No ghosts or demons, no burglars or lunatics hiding under the stair. A thin smile curved the corners of his mouth. Hell, the only one hiding under the stair was himself—

"Peekaboo," a voice behind him said.

FREE DURT

THEY WERE OUT for a Saturday drive on the county's back roads when they saw the sign. It was angled into the ground next to a rutted access lane that wound back into the hills—crudely made from a square of weathered plywood nailed to a post. The two words on it had been hand-drawn, none too neatly, with black paint.

FREE DURT

Ramage laughed out loud. "Look at that, will you? Proof positive of the dumbing-down of America."

"Oh, don't be so superior," Carolyn said. "Lots of people can't spell. That doesn't mean they're illiterate."

"D-u-r-t? A five-year-old kid can spell *dirt* correctly."

"Not everyone's had the benefits of a college education, you know. Or a cushy white-collar job."

"Cushy? Any time you want to trade, you let me know. I'd damn well rather be a school administrator than an ad-agency copywriter any day."

"Sure. At half the salary."

"Beside the point, anyway," Ramage said. "We were talking about that sign. Whoever made it couldn't've got past the first grade—that's the point."

"You can be such a snob sometimes," she said. Then: "I wonder why they're giving it away?"

"Giving what away? You mean dirt?"

"Well, out here in the country like this. Why don't they just spread it over the fields or something?"

"That's a good question."

"And where did they get so much that they have to give it away for nothing? Some kind of construction project?"

"Could be." He slowed the BMW, began looking for a place to turn around. "Let's go find out."

"Oh, now, Sam . . ."

"Why not? I'd like to know the answer myself. And I'd like to meet somebody who doesn't know how to spell *dirt.*"

She put up an argument, but he didn't pay any attention. He drove back to the rutted lane, turned into it. It meandered through a grassy meadow, up over the brow of a hill and down the other side. From the crest they could see the farm below, nestled in a wide hollow flanked on one side by a willow-banked creek and on the other by a small orchard of some kind. The layout surprised Ramage. He'd expected a little place, run-down or close to it, something out of Appalachia West. He couldn't have been more wrong.

It wasn't just that the farm was large—farmhouse, big barn, smaller barn, chicken coop, two other outbuildings, a vegetable garden, the rows of fruit trees, fences around the house and along the lane farther down and marching across the nearby fields. It was that everything was pristine. The buildings, the fences gleamed with fresh coats of white paint. The wire in the chicken run looked new. There wasn't anything in sight that seemed old or worn or out of place.

"Whoever owns this may not know how to spell," Carolyn said, "but they certainly know how to keep things in apple-pie order."

Ramage drove down between the fences and into the farmyard. A dog began to bark somewhere in the house as he nosed the BMW up near the front gate. Once he shut off the engine, the noise of the dog and the clucking of chickens and the murmur of an afternoon breeze were the only sounds.

They got out of the car. The front door of the house opened just then and a man came out with a dog on a chain leash. When Ramage got a good look at the man, he thought wryly: *Now that's more like it.* Farmer from top to bottom, like the one in the Grant Wood painting. In his sixties, tall, stringy, with a prominent Adam's apple and a face like an old, seamed baseball glove. He was even wearing overalls.

As he brought the dog out through the gate, Carolyn moved close to Ramage and a little behind him. Big dogs made her edgy. This one was pretty big, all right, some kind of Rottweiler mix, probably, but it didn't look very fierce. Just a shaggy farm dog, the only difference being that its coat was better groomed than most and it didn't make a sound now that it was leashed.

"Howdy, old-timer," Ramage said to the farmer. "How you doing?"

"Howdy yourself."

"We were driving by and saw your sign down by the road."

"Figured as much. Brings visitors up every now and then."

"I'll bet it does."

"Interested in free dirt, are you?"

"Might be."

"Can't get but a couple of sacks in that little car of yours."

"We couldn't use any more than that. You the owner here?"

"That's right. Name's Peete. Last name, three e's."

"Sam Ramage. This is my girlfriend, Carolyn White."

Carolyn gave him a look. She didn't like the word girlfriend. Ms. Feminist. But hell, that was what she was, wasn't it?

"What's the dog's name?"

"Buck."

"He doesn't bite, does he?" Carolyn asked.

"Not unless I tell him to. Or unless you try to bite him."

That made her smile. 'You have a nice place here, Mr. Peete."

"Suits me."

"Must take a lot of work to keep everything so spic-and-span."

"Does. Always something that needs tending to."

"Keeps you and your hired hands busy, I'll bet."

"Don't have any hired hands," Peete said.

"Really? Just you and your family, then."

"No family, neither."

"You mean you live here alone?"

"Me and Buck."

"Must be kind of a lonely life, way out here, if you don't mind my saying so."

"I like it. Don't like people much." Peete was looking at Ramage's right hand. "Some trick you got there, young fella," he said.

Ramage grinned. He'd been knuckle-rolling his lucky coin back and forth across the tops of his fingers, making it disappear into his palm and then reappear again on the other side.

"That's his only trick," Carolyn said. "He's so proud of it he has to show it off to everybody he meets."

"Don't pay any attention to her. *Her* only trick is running her mouth."

"Never seen a coin like that," Peete said. "What kind is it?"

"Spanish doubloon. I picked it up in the Caribbean a couple of years ago."

"Genuine?"

"Absolutely." Ramage did three more quick finger rolls, made the coin disappear into his hand and then into his pocket. "I don't see this free dirt of yours, old-timer. Where have you got it?"

"Barn yonder."

"Let's have a look."

Peete led them across the farmyard to the smaller of the two gleaming white barns, the big dog trotting silently at his side. On the way Ramage asked conversationally, "What do you keep in the big barn? Cows?"

"Don't have any cows."

"Sheep? Goats?"

"No livestock except chickens. Big barn's for storage."

"Farm equipment?"

"Among other things."

When they reached the smaller barn, Peete unlatched the double doors and swung one of the halves open. Ramage could smell the dirt before he saw it, a kind of heavy, loamy odor in the gloom. It was piled high between a pair of tall wood partitions, not as much as he'd expected, but a pretty large hunk of real estate just the same—ten feet long, maybe twenty feet deep, by seven or eight feet high. He moved closer. Mixture of clods and loose earth, all dark brown with reddish highlights. Some of it toward the bottom had a crusty look, as if it had been there for a while; the rest seemed more or less fresh.

"What makes this dirt so special?" he asked the farmer.

"Special?"

"Well, there's a lot of it, and you keep it in here instead of outside, and you give it away free. How come?"

"Best there is. Rich. Good for gardens, lawns."

"So why don't you use it yourself, on that vegetable garden behind the house?"

"I do. Got more than I need."

"Where does it come from?" Carolyn asked. "Someplace on your property?"

"Yep. Truck it in from the cemetery."

She blinked. "From the . . . did you say cemetery?"

"That's right. It's graveyard dirt."

There was a little silence before Ramage said, "You're kidding."

"No, sir. Gospel truth."

"Graveyard dirt."

"Yep."

"From a cemetery on your property."

"Yep. Old Indian burial ground."

"Never heard of any Indian tribes around here."

"Long time ago. Miwoks."

Carolyn asked, "You don't desecrate the graves, do you? Just so you can carry off a lot of rich soil?"

"Nope. Do my digging in the cemetery, but not where the graves are."

"How can you be sure?"

"I'm sure. You would be, too, if you saw the place."

"Miwoks?" Ramage said. "I didn't think they ranged this far south."

"Nomadic bunch, must've been."

"Nomads don't build cemeteries for their dead."

Peete fixed him with a squinty look. "Don't believe there's a burial ground close-by, that it?"

"Let's just say I'm skeptical."

"Prove it to you, if you want," Peete said. "Take you over and show it to you."

"Yeah? How far away is it?"

"Not far. Won't take long."

Ramage looked at Carolyn. "Oh, no," she said, "count me out."

"Real interesting spot," Peete said. "Artifacts and things."

"What kind of artifacts?" Ramage asked.

"Arrowheads, bowls, pots. Just lying around."

"Uh-huh."

"Fact. See for yourself."

"Not me," Carolyn said. "I don't like cemeteries. And I've seen all the Native American artifacts I care to see."

"No damn spirit of adventure," Ramage said.

"You go ahead if you want. I'm staying right here."

She meant it. And when she got stubborn about something, you couldn't change her mind for love or money.

Ramage said disgustedly, "All right, the hell with it. I guess we'll have to take your word for it, old-timer. About the dirt and the burial ground, both."

"Some do, some don't. Suit yourself."

"For now, anyway," he added. "Maybe some other time."

"Any time you want to see it." Peete gestured at the pile of free dirt. "How many sacks you want?"

"None right now. Some other time on that, too."

Peete shrugged, led them out of the barn into the sunshine. He closed the doors, set the latch, and started to move off.

"Hold on a second," Ramage said. And when the farmer stopped and glanced back at him, "About that sign of yours, down by the road."

"What about it?"

"Don't take offense, but you misspelled *dirt.*"

"That a fact?"

"It's with an 'i,' not a 'u.' D-i-r-t. You might want to correct it."

"Then again," Peete said, "I might not."

He took the dog away to the house without a backward glance.

Carolyn said, "Did you have to bring up that sign?"

Ramage ignored her until they were in the car, bouncing down the rutted lane. Then he said, more to himself than to her, "Some character, that Peete."

"You think he's just a dumb hick, I suppose."

"Don't you?"

"No. I think he's a lot smarter than you give him credit for."

"Because of that business with the dirt and the Indian burial ground? I didn't believe it for a minute."

"Well, neither did I," she said. "That's the real reason I didn't want to go along with him. The whole thing's a hoax, a game he plays with gullible tourists. I wouldn't be surprised if he misspelled *dirt* on that sign just to draw people like us up here."

"Might have at that."

"If we'd gone along with him, what he'd have shown us is some spot he faked up with Native American artifacts and phony graves."

"Just to get a good laugh at our expense?"

"Some people have a warped sense of humor."

"Didn't look like Peete had any sense of humor."

"You can't tell what a person's like inside from the face they wear in public. You ought to know that."

"I'd still like to've seen the place," Ramage said.

"Why, for heaven's sake?"

"Satisfy my curiosity."

"You'd've been playing right into his hand."

"Still. I can't help being curious, can I?"

He stayed curious all that day, and the next, and the next after that. About the fake Miwok burial ground, and about Peete, too. How could the old buzzard afford to pay for all the upkeep on that farm of his, and give away good rich soil, when he had no help and no livestock except for a few chickens? Crops like alfalfa, fruit from that small orchard? Maybe he ought to drive back out there, alone this time, and have a look at the "cemetery" and see what else he could find out.

On Friday afternoon, Ramage decided that that was just what he was going to do.

The snotty young fella named Coolidge said, "I don't believe it."

"Gospel truth."

"Graveyard dirt from some old Indian cemetery?"

"Every inch of it."

"And you truck it in here and hoard it so you can give it away free. You think I was born yesterday, Pop?"

"Prove it to you, if you want."

"How you going to do that?"

"Burial ground's not far from here," Peete said. "Other side of that hill yonder."

"And you want me to go see it with you."

"Up to you. Only take a few minutes."

Coolidge thought about it. Then he grinned crookedly and said, "All right, for free d-u-r-t, why not? What have I got to lose?"

"That's right," Peete said. He tightened his grip on Buck's chain, tossed his new lucky piece into the air with his other hand. Sunlight struck golden glints from the doubloon before he caught it with a quick downward swipe. "What have you got to lose?"

JUST LOOKING

H E HADN'T HAD a woman in so long, he'd started carrying a picture of his right hand around in his wallet.

Everybody he told that to, the guys he worked with at Mossman Hardware, his buddies at the Starlite Tavern, thought it was a pretty funny line. He laughed right along with them. But at night, alone in his two-room apartment, he didn't think it was so funny anymore. Thing was, it was the plain damn truth. He'd only had a couple of women in his entire life—thirty-four years old and been laid just twice, both of those times with hookers. Last time had been over eight years ago. He was just too embarrassed to get undressed in front of some hard-shell whore in a lighted room, have her look at him naked and see the contempt and laughter in her eyes. Too painful, man.

The way he figured it now, he'd never have sex again unless he paid for it. Never get married, never have the kind of relationship other guys had with a woman. He was too butt-ugly. No getting away from that—he had mirrors in his apartment, he saw his reflection in store windows, he knew what he looked like. Big puffy body on little stubby legs, not much chin, mouth like a razor slash, knobby head with a patch of hair like moss growing on a tree stump. Somebody'd said that to him once, in the Starlite or someplace. "You know something, man? You got a head looks like moss growing on a fuckin' tree stump."

Most of the time it didn't bother him too much, being a toad and not having a woman. Most of the time he was a pretty happy guy. He liked his job at Mossman Hardware, he liked drinking and shooting pool with his buddies, he liked baseball (even if some of the players nowadays with their billion-dollar contracts were assholes), he liked bowling at Freedom Lanes and playing draw poker at Henson's Card Room and watching martial arts flicks on the tube and now and then reading a Louis L'Amour western if he was in the mood for a good book. And when he got horny, well, he had his collection of porn videos and he could go on the Net and surf through the porn sites. Looking was the next best thing to having, right? Just looking could be pretty damn good.

But sometimes, some nights, not having a woman really bothered him. Some nights he felt like busting down and bawling. Life sucked sometimes. When you had a face and a body like his, when you looked like you'd been whupped with an ugly stick, life really *sucked* sometimes.

He figured things would go on pretty much as they always had, the good and the bad, right up until he croaked. One day the same as another. Weekdays he went to work at the hardware store, knocked off at six, headed to the Starlite or Freedom Lanes or Henson's, went home and watched a video or fooled around online and then went to bed. Weekends he took in a ballgame, holed up in the Starlite, played poker, played pool, played with his computer, played with himself. Boring, sure, but he was used to it and mostly it suited him. He was better off than a lot of poor jobless schmucks living on the streets or on welfare or hooked on drugs, wasn't he?

Yeah. Sure he was.

Only then, all at once, everything changed.

Then he met Julie Brock.

Well, he didn't really meet her. More like he ran into her, almost. It was on a Saturday morning and he was in Safeway buying a couple of six-packs and some TV dinners and other stuff. He pushed his cart around into the frozen food aisle, and there she was, not two feet away, so that he had to veer off to avoid slamming his cart into hers. As soon as he got a good look at her, it was like he'd been punched in the belly. He couldn't catch his breath, couldn't stop staring. He must've looked like one of those cartoon characters, Wile E. Coyote or Bugs Bunny, when they got surprised—tongue hanging loose, eyes bugged out so far it was like they were on the end of stalks.

She was a blonde. Not your ordinary blonde, not your Marilyn Monroe type. Sort of a tawny blonde, dark and light at the same time, he'd never seen a color like it. And tall, real tall, almost six feet, with perfect bare legs that went up and up and up. Nice little rack, nice tight ass. Oh, she was gorgeous, man, the sweetest piece of sweetmeat he'd ever feasted his eyes on. She knew it, too. Walked slow and lazy, like a cat, her head up and her nose up. Haughty. Sweet and haughty and twice as sexy in a pair of shorts and a blouse as any of the naked broads on the Net or humping in one of his porn flicks.

She didn't pay any attention to him, didn't even glance at him. She stopped pushing her cart and opened a freezer case and bent over to get something off one of the lower shelves so he had an even better view of her ass. He stood there staring until she moved on. Then he started pushing his cart after her. He couldn't stop looking, he couldn't just let her go away. He felt like he'd died and gone to heaven. He felt like . . . he didn't know *what* he felt like, except that he was all hot and cold inside and his Johnson was half standing at attention in his shorts.

He followed her around the store, not real close so's she or anybody else would notice. He got in the same checkout line she did. He trailed her out to the parking lot, to a little red Miata. His own beat-up wheels were in the next row. He hustled over there and threw his bags in the backseat, and when she pulled out of the lot he was right behind her.

This is crazy, he thought after a few blocks. Me following a woman around, any woman, let alone a stone fox like her. But what the hell, it wasn't like he was a pervert or anything. He didn't mean her any harm. All he was doing was *looking.*

So he kept on following her, all the way home. And it turned out she lived in a bungalow on Acacia Street, five blocks from his apartment. He parked across the street and watched her carry her groceries inside, and he had a big urge to go over there, offer to help so he could see her again up close. But he didn't give in to it because he knew what'd happen if he did. She'd take one look at him and tell him to bugger off. She probably had a dozen handsome guys sniffing after her every day, she might even be married or living with somebody. She wouldn't want anything to do with a butt-ugly toad with a head that looked like moss growing on a fuckin' tree stump.

She took the last grocery bag into the bungalow and didn't come out again. He stayed put for a while, but he couldn't keep on sitting there all day waiting for another look. That was just plain stupid. So he drove on to his apartment and put his groceries away and sat down in his recliner. He'd planned to go to a ballgame today, Giants were playing the Dodgers, but now he didn't feel like it. Didn't feel like bowling or going to the Starlite or doing anything else he liked to do on Saturdays.

He couldn't stop thinking about the blonde. It was like she was lodged inside his head, big as life, that tawny light-and-dark hair and that gorgeous face and that hard body.

Oh, that fine, hard body!

Sunday morning he drove over to Acacia Street again. He'd dreamed about her that night, damn near a wet dream, and woke up with her, and wanted to see her again in the flesh so bad he couldn't think about anything else.

Damn, though—her Miata wasn't in the driveway. He parked and waited a half hour or so, but she didn't come home. He got tired of just sitting and walked over in front of her place, casual, like a guy out for a Sunday stroll. Her bungalow was small, painted a bright blue with white trim, trees and bushes growing thick along both sides. When he squinted down the driveway he could see a jungly backyard, too—part of a lawn, more trees, some tall oleanders. He knew this neighborhood almost as well as his own and he was pretty sure the yard butted up close to Miller Creek.

Back in his car, he drove around the block. Two blocks, matter of fact, because what was behind her place was a grammar school. Nobody was at the school today except some kids playing basketball on the courts behind the classrooms. He walked past them, across a soccer field and another acre or so of lawn. A chainlink fence made up the far boundary. On the other side of that was Miller Creek, and on the other side of the creek was the blue bungalow. He could see part of its ass end when he got to the fence, but the rest was hidden by the trees and oleanders.

Another thing he could see was that it was a short distance down the bank, across the mostly dry creekbed, and up the other bank into those bushes. Be easy enough to find your way in the dark if you were careful. You wouldn't need to climb the fence, either. There was a gate about twenty yards away. Why they'd put a gate in the fence here was anybody's guess, but there it was. The padlock on it was an old Schindler. He grinned when he saw that. Hell, with one of the passkeys they had at Mossman Hardware, you could open that puppy up in about two seconds flat.

Eight o'clock Monday morning, he was back across the street from the blue bungalow. He didn't have to be at work until ten and he was hoping the blonde would leave for whatever job she had long before that. Sure enough, she came out at about eight-twenty. All dressed up in a tan suit, that tawny blonde hair piled high on top of her head. Sweetmeat for a treat!

He followed her red Miata downtown. She stopped for coffee and a doughnut or something at a bakery on Fourth and then she went to the Merchants' Exchange Bank on Hollowell. The bank wasn't open yet, but somebody let her in and she didn't come out again. So that had to be where she worked.

He took another ride to the bank on his lunch hour, and this time he went inside. He saw her right away. She wasn't a teller—she had her own desk and she was tapping away on a computer, her lower lip caught between her teeth. He tried not to stare too hard as he walked by. There was one of those little nameplates on her desk and that was how he found out her name was Julie Brock.

Over the next week he found out some more things about her, just by hanging around the bank and her neighborhood. Turned out she wasn't married or living with anybody. She did have a boyfriend, handsome football player type who drove a fuckin' Mercedes. The boyfriend stayed late at her bungalow a couple of times, but not the whole night. Which maybe meant *he* was married, or maybe it didn't mean anything at all. Guy didn't come over every night, either, only on Friday and Saturday. During the week, she turned out her lights and hit the sack before eleven. Probably because she had to get up early for her job.

The following Monday night, he left his apartment a little before ten and drove to the grammar school. He made sure nobody was around before he went into the schoolyard, across to the chainlink fence. He was scared and excited, both. He knew he was taking a real big risk, he'd had a lot of conversations with himself about that, but he hadn't been able to talk himself out of it. Crazy, sure, but it was the only way he'd ever get to see her alone, up close and personal.

He slipped through the gate, picked his way across the creek and up into her yard without making enough noise to carry. The rear windows and back entrance were dark, but he found a lighted window on the far side. The curtains were open and the room inside was plain as day. Oh, man, it was her bedroom! She wasn't in there, but the covers on the bed were turned down and more light was showing behind a partly open door in the far wall.

He stepped into a patch of tree shadow, his mouth dry and metal-tasting. It was a perfect spot for looking, only about twenty-five feet of lawn between him and the window. He waited there, so damn excited he had trouble catching his breath.

And then he heard the sound of a toilet flushing and she walked out of the bathroom, and all she was wearing was a bra and panties. Bug-eyed, he watched her move around here and there, arranging clothes and stuff. And then she started doing a bunch of exercises, bending over, stretching, jumping, twisting, all that fine glistening flesh shaking and quivering.

He didn't think the show could get any better, but pretty soon it did. As soon as she stopped exercizing, she reached up behind her and unhooked her bra and let it fall. A couple of seconds later she was out of her panties, too. Natural blonde! He couldn't believe he was seeing her like that, all of her, naked. Hot and sweaty and na- ked, right there in front of him, rubbing her hands under her breasts and down over her hips . . .

Man, oh, man, oh man oh man oh man ohmanohmanohman- ohmanohman—oh!

He kept going back there. After that show the first night, he wouldn't've stayed away for a million bucks. Didn't go Friday or Saturday, but most every other night. Once the boyfriend was there even though it wasn't the weekend, the two together in the sack, but the only light was in the bathroom and he couldn't see much of what they were doing. Another time she had the curtains closed for some damn reason. The rest of the nights it was show- time. Into the bedroom she'd come in bra and panties, fuss around, do those exercises for about ten minutes, get naked, rub up that hot sweaty body for a minute or so, then go take a shower and get into bed and shut off the light. Man, it was better than any video he'd ever seen, porn or otherwise.

Then one night, a real warm night, she had the bedroom win- dow open for some air. She came out and did her number, and he must've shifted around and made a noise or something because all of a sudden she quit exercizing and moved to the window and stood peering out. He was pretty sure she couldn't see him out in the dark, but he froze anyway. She stood staring for a few seconds and then, quick, she shut the window and went and turned out the light before she got into bed.

He should've taken that as a warning and not gone back for a while. But he didn't. He went back the next night at the same time.

And that was his big mistake.

The lights were on in her bedroom, same as usual, but he didn't see her as he slipped through the oleanders to his ringside spot. He figured she was still in the bathroom, which was always a relief because a time or two he'd got there a little late and missed part of the show. He eased forward into the patch of tree shadow, licking his lips.

And all of a sudden a bright beam of light hit him square in the eyes and a voice, her voice, said hard and angry, "You dirty damn pervert!"

He almost jumped out of his skin. Panic surged in him and he'd've taken off, run like the fuckin' wind if she hadn't said, "Stand right there—I have a gun, I'll shoot if you move."

He froze. Heard himself say, "A gun?" in a voice like a frog croaking.

"That's right, and I know how to use it. You don't think I'd be out here waiting for you unarmed, do you?"

"Listen, I'm sorry, Julie, I didn't mean nothing—"

"Oh, so you know my name. Well, I know *you,* too, you fat creep, I've seen you before. What were you planning to do? Sneak in some night and rape me?"

"No! Jesus, no, I never would've done nothing like that, I never would've hurt you . . ."

"You just like to watch, is that it? Well, your Peeping Tom days are over right now."

"What . . . what're you gonna do?"

"Call the police, that's what I'm going to do."

"No, wait, you can't—"

"Can't I? You just watch me. Go on, get moving."

"Moving? Where?"

"Into the house, where do you think?"

He didn't want to go into the house. He still wanted to run, but what good would that do? She could identify him, she'd sic the cops on him anyway—

"Move, I said. If you don't do what I say, if you try anything, I'll shoot you. I mean it, I will."

For a few seconds more it was like he was paralyzed. Then he wasn't anymore, his legs were moving and taking him out onto the lawn. The flashlight glare slid out of his eyes—she was over on the other side of the tree—but he was still half blind. He stumbled and heard somebody make a little moaning sound . . . him, it came out of *him.* She told him to walk around to the back door and he did that. She told him to open it and go inside and he did that, too.

Kitchen. He stood there blinking, trying to focus, so scared he was shaking all over. She came in behind him, looped around to one of those breakfast bar counters a few feet away. She had a gun, all right. Little silver automatic that caught the light and seemed to be winking at him.

"Sit down at the table over there," she said.

Still blinking, he started over to the table. Then he stopped and
swung his head toward her again. Now she had a cordless phone in
her other hand. Her eyes shifted back and forth between him and
the phone, her face all scrunched up and hot-eyed, and she wasn't
the most beautiful woman he'd ever seen anymore, she wasn't
even pretty, she was a hag as ugly as he was getting ready to have
him arrested, put in prison—

He lunged at her. Didn't think about what he was doing, just
did it. She swung the gun up and squeezed the trigger point blank.
She'd've killed him sure, shot him down like a dog, except that the
little automatic must've jammed because it didn't go off, and in
the next second he was on her.

He knocked the gun out of her hand, yanked the phone away
from her. She opened up her mouth to scream. He jammed his
hand over it, dragged her body in tight against his. Even then, even
after she'd tried to blow his brains out, he didn't have any idea of
hurting her, only wanted to keep her from yelling somehow so he
could get away. But she fought and squirmed, kicking his shins,
clawing his arm, it was like he had hold of a wildcat. She got one
arm all the way loose and those long nails slashed up and ripped
furrows in his neck. That hurt, really hurt. Made him mad and kind
of wild himself. He couldn't hold her, and she twisted her body
and pulled loose and tried to break his balls with her knee.

The next thing he knew he was hitting her with the phone. Hitting her, hitting her, hitting her until she quit making noises and
quit fighting and fell down on the floor on her back. There was
blood all over her face and head and her eyes were wide open with
a lot of the white showing. He saw that and he wasn't wild anymore. He stared at her, stared at the blood, stared at the bloody
phone in his hand. He made the same kind of sound he'd made
outside and dropped the phone and went down on one knee beside
her. Picked up one of her wrists—limp, no pulse—and put his fingers against her neck and didn't feel any pulse there, either.

Dead!

Then he ran. Ran like there was a pack of junkyard dogs on his
heels. Out of the kitchen, across the yard, through the bushes,
across the creek, through the fence gate, across the schoolyard and
out to where he'd parked his wheels. Not caring how much noise
he made or if anybody saw him, not caring about anything except
getting far away from there.

He didn't remember driving home. He was running and then he
was at the car and then he was in his apartment putting on the dead

bolt and the chain lock. He was shaking so hard he could hear a clicking sound, his teeth knocking together or maybe the bones rattling inside his skin. When he put on the light he saw blood on his hands, on his shirt and jacket. He ripped all his clothes off and got into the shower and scrubbed and scrubbed, but he couldn't make himself feel clean. He couldn't get warm, either, not even lying in bed with the electric blanket turned all the way up.

He lay there in the dark, his head full of pictures of her lying on her kitchen floor all bloody and dead. But it wasn't his fault. She'd tried to kill him, hadn't she? Clawed him, tried to break his balls? He hadn't wanted to hurt her—she'd made him do it in self-defense. Her fault, not his. Hers, hers, hers!

He kept listening for the doorbell. Waiting for the cops to come. He'd tell them it wasn't his fault, but he knew they'd take him to jail anyway.

Only the cops didn't come. He lay wide awake the whole night, waiting, and in the morning he was amazed he was still alone.

He called up his boss, Mr. Mossman, and said he was sick, he wouldn't be in today. Then he put on his robe and sat in his recliner with the TV going for noise and waited for the cops to show up.

All day he sat there and still no cops.

At six o'clock he switched over to the news and pretty soon he heard her name, saw her picture flash on the screen. Julie Brock, twenty-seven, found dead in her rented bungalow on Acacia Street, bludgeoned to death with a cordless phone. Neighbors had heard noises, one of them saw a man running away but couldn't describe him because it'd been too dark. The TV guy said the police were working on several leads and expected to make an arrest soon. Maybe that was the truth and maybe it wasn't. All he could do was sit scared, wait scared to find out.

He waited four whole days, there in the apartment the whole time. Told Mr. Mossman he had the flu and Mr. Mossman said take care of himself, get plenty of rest, drink plenty of liquids. He drank plenty of liquids, all right. Beer, wine, scotch, every kind of alcohol he had in the place. Watched TV, drank, threw up most of what he ate, and waited.

The cops never did show up.

On the fifth day he wasn't so scared anymore. On the sixth day he was hardly scared at all and he went out for the first time to buy some more beer and booze. On the seventh day he knew they weren't going to come and arrest him, not ever. He couldn't say how he knew that, he just did.

The furrows on his neck were mostly healed by then, but he put on a high-necked shirt and buttoned the top button to make sure the marks didn't show. Then he went back to work. Mr. Mossman said it was good to have him back. That night, when he went to the Starlite Tavern, his buddies said the same thing and bought him a couple of rounds of drinks and he won eight bucks shooting pool.

Things settled down to normal again. He worked and went to the Starlite and Freedom Lanes and Henson's Card Room, the same as he used to, and the whole crazy thing with Julie Brock faded and faded until he wasn't thinking about her at all anymore. It was as if none of it ever happened. Not just that last night in her bungalow—all the nights before it, the whole crazy business. He couldn't even remember what she looked like.

A lot more time passed, and his life was just the way it'd been before, good sometimes, boring sometimes, lonely sometimes. And then one day he was working behind the counter at the hardware store and he looked up and this babe was standing there. A redhead—oh, man, the most gorgeous redhead he'd ever seen. His eyes bugged out like they were on stalks. Young, slim, that red hair like fire around her head, white skin smooth as cream, a great rack poking out the front of her sweater, her mouth big and soft and smiling at him. He stared and stared, but she didn't stop smiling. Real friendly type, wanted to buy a space heater and some other stuff for her new apartment.

He showed her around, helped her pick out the best items, wrote up her order. She wanted to know could she have it delivered, and he said sure, you bet, and she gave him her address along with her credit card. He watched her walk out, the way her ass swung under her green skirt, and his mouth was dry and he felt all hot and cold inside and his Johnson was having fits in his shorts.

He couldn't stop thinking about her all day. She was the most beautiful, exciting woman he'd ever feasted his eyes on. Before he got off work he packed up her order so he could deliver it himself, personally. He had to see her again, see where she lived.

There wasn't any harm in that, was there? Just looking?

A COLD FOGGY DAY

THE TWO MEN stepped off the Boston-to-San Francisco plane at two o'clock on a cold foggy afternoon in February. The younger of the two by several years had sand-colored hair and a small birthmark on his right cheek; the older man had flat gray eyes and heavy black brows. Both wore topcoats and carried small overnight bags.

They walked through the terminal and down to one of the rental-car agencies on the lower level. The older man paid for the rental of a late-model sedan. When they stepped outside, the wind was blowing and the wall of fog eddied in gray waves across the airport complex. The younger man thrust his hands deep into the pockets of his topcoat as they crossed to the lot where the rental cars were kept. He could not remember when he had been quite so cold.

A boy in a white uniform brought their car around. The older man took the wheel. As he pulled the car out of the lot, the younger man said, "Turn the heater on, will you, Harry? I'm freezing in here."

Harry put on the heater. Warm air rushed against their feet, but it would be a long while before it was warm enough to suit the younger man. He sat blowing on his hands. "Is it always this cold out here?" he asked.

"It's not cold," Harry said.

"Well, I'm freezing."

"It's just the fog, Vince. You're not used to it."

"There's six inches of snow in Boston," Vince said. "Ice on the streets thick enough to skate on. But I'm damned if it's as cold as it is out here."

"You have to get used to it."

"I don't think I *could* get used to it," Vince said. "It cuts through you like a knife."

"The sun comes out around noon most days and burns off the fog," Harry said. "San Francisco has the mildest winters you've ever seen."

The younger man didn't say anything more. He didn't want to argue with Harry; this was Harry's home town. How could you argue with a man about his home town?

When they reached San Francisco, 20 minutes later, Harry drove a roundabout route to their hotel. It was an old but elegant place on Telegraph Hill, and the windows in their room had a panoramic view of the bay. Even with the fog, you could see the Golden Gate Bridge and the Bay Bridge and Alcatraz Island. Harry pointed out each of them.

But Vince was still cold and he said he wanted to take a hot shower. He stood under a steaming spray for ten minutes. When he came out again, Harry was still standing at the windows.

"Look at that view," Harry said, "Isn't that some view?"

"Sure," Vince agreed. "Some view."

"San Francisco is a beautiful city, Vince. It's the most beautiful city in the world."

"Then why did you ever leave it? Why did you come to Boston? You don't seem too happy there."

"Ambition," Harry said. "I had a chance to move up and I took it. But it's been a long time, Vince."

"You could always move back here."

"I'm going to do that," Harry said. "Now that I'm home again, I know I don't want to live anywhere else. I tell you, this is the most beautiful city anywhere on this earth."

Vince was silent. He wished Harry wouldn't keep talking about how beautiful San Francisco was. Vince liked Boston; it was his town just as San Francisco was Harry's. But Vince couldn't see talking about it all the time, the way Harry had ever since they'd left Boston this morning. Not that Vince would say anything about it. Harry had been around a long time and Vince was just a new man. He didn't know Harry that well—had only worked with him a few times; but everybody said you could learn a lot from him. And Vince wanted to learn.

That was not the only reason he wouldn't say anything about it. Vince knew why Harry was talking so much about San Francisco. It was to keep his mind off the job they had come here to do. Still, it probably wasn't doing him much good, or Vince any good either. The only way to take both their minds off the job was to get it done.

"When are we going after him, Harry?" Vince said.

"Tonight."

"Why not now?"

"Because I say so. We'll wait until tonight."

"Listen, Harry—"

"We're doing this my way, remember?" Harry said. "That was the agreement. *My* way."

"All right," Vince said, but he was beginning to feel more and more nervous about this whole thing with Dominic DiLucci. He wished it was over and finished with and he was back in Boston with his wife. Away from Harry.

After a while Harry suggested they go out to Fisherman's Wharf and get something to eat. Vince wasn't hungry and he didn't want to go to Fisherman's Wharf; all he wanted to do was to get the job over and done with. But Harry insisted, so he gave in. It was better to humor Harry than to complicate things by arguing with him.

They took a cable car to Fisherman's Wharf and walked around there for a time, in the fog and the chill wind. Vince was almost numb by the time Harry picked out a restaurant, but Harry didn't seem to be affected by the weather at all. He didn't even have his topcoat buttoned.

Harry sat by the window in the restaurant, not eating much, looking out at the fishing boats moored in the Wharf basin. He had his face close to the glass, like a kid.

Vince watched him and thought: He's stalling. Well, Vince could understand that, but understanding it didn't make it any easier. He said finally, "Harry, it's after seven. There's no sense in putting it off any longer."

Harry sighed. "I guess you're right."

"Sure I am."

"All right," Harry said.

He wanted to take the cable car back to their hotel, but Vince said it was too cold riding on one of those things. So they caught a taxi, and then picked up their rental car. Vince turned on the heater himself this time, as high as it would go.

Once they had turned out of the hotel garage, Vince said, "Where is he, Harry? You can tell me that now."

"Down the coast. Outside Pacifica."

"How far is that?"

"About twenty miles."

"Suppose he's not there?"

"He'll be there."

"I don't see how you can be so sure."

"He'll be there," Harry said.

"He could be in Mexico by now."

"He's not in Mexico," Harry said. "He's in a little cabin outside Pacifica."

Vince shrugged and decided not to press the point. This was Harry's show; he himself was along only as a back-up.

Harry drove them out to Golden Gate Park and through it and eventually onto the Coast Highway, identifying landmarks that were half hidden in fog. Vince didn't pay much attention; he was trying to forget his own nervousness by thinking about his wife back in Boston.

It took them almost an hour to get where they were going. Harry drove through Pacifica and beyond it several miles. Then he turned right, toward the ocean, onto a narrow dirt road that wound steadily upward through gnarled cypress and eucalyptus trees. That's what Harry said they were anyway. There was fog here too, thick and gray and roiling. Vince could almost feel the coldness of it, as if it were seeping into the car through the vents.

They passed several cabins, most of them dark, a couple with warm yellow light showing at the windows. Harry turned onto another road, pitted and dark, and after a few hundred yards they rounded a bend. Vince could see another cabin then. It was small and dark, perched on the edge of a cliff that fell away to the ocean. But the water was hidden by the thick fog.

Harry parked the car near the front door of the cabin. He shut off the engine and the headlights.

Vince said, "I don't see any lights."

"That doesn't mean anything."

"It doesn't look like he's here."

"He'll be here."

Vince didn't say anything. He didn't see how Harry could know with that much certainty that Dominic DiLucci was going to be here. You just didn't know anybody that well.

They left the warmth of the car. The wind was sharp and stinging, blowing across the top of the bluff from the sea. Vince shivered.

Harry knocked on the cabin door and they stood waiting. And after a few moments the door opened and a thin man with haunted eyes looked out. He was dressed in rumpled slacks and a white shirt that was soiled around the collar. He hadn't shaved in several days.

The man stood looking at Harry and didn't seem surprised to see him. At length he said, "Hello, Harry."

"Hello, Dom," Harry said.

They continued to look at each other. Dominic DiLucci said, "Well, it's cold out there." His voice was calm, controlled, but empty, as if there was no emotion left inside him. "Why don't you come in?"

They entered the cabin. A fire glowed on a brick hearth against one wall. Dom switched on a small lamp in the front room, and Vince saw that the furniture there was old and overstuffed, a man's furniture. He stood apart from the other two men, thinking that Harry had been right all along and that it wouldn't be long before the job was finished. But for some reason that didn't make him feel any less nervous. Or any less cold.

Harry said, "You don't seem surprised to see me, Dom."

"Surprised?" Dom said. "No, I'm not surprised. Nothing can surprise me any more."

"It's been a long time. You haven't changed much."

"Haven't I?" Dom said, and smiled a cold humorless smile.

"No," Harry said. "You came here. I knew you would. You always came here when you were troubled, when you wanted to get away from something."

Dominic DiLucci was silent.

Harry said, "Why did you do it, Dom?"

"Why? Because of Trudy, that's why."

"I don't follow that. I thought she'd left you, run off with somebody from Los Angeles."

"She did. But I love her, Harry, and I wanted her back. I thought I could buy her back with the money. I thought if I got in touch with her and told her I had a hundred thousand dollars, she'd come back and we could go off to Brazil or someplace."

"But she didn't come back, did she?"

"No. She called me a fool and a loser on the phone and hung up on me. I didn't know what to do then. The money didn't mean much without Trudy; nothing means much without her. Maybe I wanted to be caught after that, maybe that's why I stayed around here. And maybe you figured that out about me along with everything else."

"That's right," Harry said. "Trudy was right, too, you know. You *are* a fool and a loser, Dom."

"Is that all you have to say?"

"What do you want me to say?"

"Nothing, I guess. It's about what I expected from you. You have no feelings, Harry. There's nothing inside of you and there never was or will be."

Dom rubbed a hand across his face, and the hand was trembling. Harry just watched him. Vince watched him too, and he thought that Dominic DiLucci was about ready to crack; he was trying to bring it off as if he were in perfect control of himself, but he was ready to crack.

Vince said, "We'd better get going."

Dom glanced at him, the first time he had looked at him since they'd come inside. It didn't seem to matter to him who Vince was. "Yes," he said. "I suppose we'd better."

"Where's the money?" Harry asked him.

"In the bedroom. In a suitcase in the closet."

Vince went into the bedroom, found the suitcase, and looked inside. Then he closed it and came out into the front room again. Harry and Dom were no longer looking at each other.

They went outside and got into the rental car. Harry took the wheel again. Vince sat in the rear seat with Dominic DiLucci.

They drove back down to the Coast Highway and turned north toward San Francisco. They rode in silence. Vince was still cold, but he could feel perspiration under his arms. He glanced over at Dom beside him, sitting there with his hands trembling in his lap. From then on he kept his eyes on Harry.

When they came into San Francisco, Harry drove them up a winding avenue that led to the top of Twin Peaks. The fog had lifted somewhat, and from up there you could see the lights of the city strung out like misty beads along the bay.

As soon as the lights came into view Harry leaned forward, staring intently through the windshield. "Look at those lights," he said. "Magnificent. Isn't that the most magnificent sight you ever saw, Vince?"

And Vince understood then. All at once, in one stinging bite of perception, he understood the truth.

After Dominic DiLucci had stolen the $100,000 from the investment firm where he worked, Harry had told the San Francisco police that he didn't know where Dom could be. But then he had gone to the head of the big insurance company where he and Vince were both claims investigators—the same insurance company that handled the policy on Dom's investment firm— and had told the Chief that maybe he did have an idea where Dom was but hadn't said anything to the police because he wanted to come out here himself, wanted to bring Dom in himself. Dom wasn't dangerous, he said; there wouldn't be any trouble.

The Chief hadn't liked the idea much, but he wanted the $100,000 recovered. So he had paid Harry's way to San Francisco, and Vince's way with him as a back-up man. Both Vince and the Chief had figured they knew why Harry wanted to come himself. But they had been wrong. Dead wrong.

Harry DiLucci was still staring out at the lights of San Francisco. And he was smiling.

What kind of man are you? Vince thought. What kind of man sits there with his own brother in the back seat, on the way to jail and ready to crack—his own brother—and looks out at the lights of a city and smiles?

Vince shivered. This time it had nothing to do with the cold.

THE NIGHT, THE RIVER

The night, the river.
And the girl he loved.
Janine.

He sat waiting for her on the sloping bank, as he always did on warm nights like this one. Soft grass, soft breeze, soft darkness all around. The river like black glass, wide here, wide and deep and fringed with reeds. The moon painting its surface with bands of shimmery light. Thrum of crickets, a nighthawk whickering in one of the willows farther down. Sweet scents—clover, wildflowers. Even the slow-moving water, the reeds, smelled sweet on nights like this.

His home, his world. The river, the little town beyond the rail-road bridge, the countryside, the solitude. Most people his age who'd grown up here couldn't wait to get out. That was how Janine felt, always talking about going away to San Francisco or Los Angeles, New York, London. Not him. He didn't like cities, he didn't drink much or do drugs, he didn't want anything to do with wild parties or any of the crazy stuff that went on in cities. There were enough pleasures right here. Weekend dances and socials at the rec center. Boat rides, fishing trips. Hikes in the hills and valleys. And warm nights on the grassy riverbank. Janine hardly ever talked about going away when they were here, in this secret spot where they'd first vowed their love and lost their virginity together.

He thought of how she would look when she came tonight. Skin like finely veined alabaster—white. Wearing her favorite swimsuit, one piece—black. Lean, coltish body, those wonderful long legs. Shoulder-length dark hair that was silk-smooth beneath his fingers. That shy-bold smile just for him. Whispered words just for him.

"Janine," he said aloud.

Night whispers answered him. But it wouldn't be long now. He felt her nearness, out there in the dark. It was as if all he had to do to summon her was say her name.

Five minutes, maybe less. Beyond the reeds, the black glass fragmented into faint ripples that glistened in the moonshine. He sat forward, watching for the ebon shape of her head to break the surface. He would see her before he heard her. She swam so well, so quietly and effortlessly. A mile upriver from her home beyond the ruins of Miller's Ferry, a mile back down—all that distance, two or three nights a week, and not once had the swim tired her or left her winded. Born to the river, that was Janine. She'd said so herself, before all that nonsense about big cities had come into her head. "I'd much rather swim than walk, much rather be in the water than on dry land. Except when I'm with you."

There. Coming now.

Excitement built in him, drying his mouth. His gaze was avid as she floated in toward the bank. She came straight through the reeds, not avoiding them as most swimmers would, rising up out of them, dripping, like a black-and-white water sprite. When she reached the shore, she stood for a moment as if posing for him, shaking herself, tossing the wet hair from her eyes. Then, in that slow, shy way of hers, she came to him through the sweet-smelling grass.

"Janine."

The special smile, the whisper of his name, and she sat down beside him. "Have you been waiting long this time?"

"No. Just a few minutes."

"I don't like to keep you waiting."

"I know. I know you don't."

"But I'm here now. I always come, don't I, when I know you're waiting."

"You always do."

Her smile turned mischievous. "And you're always glad to see me."

"Always."

"So you can make love to me."

"That's not the only reason."

"Isn't it?"

"I just. . . I love you, you know that."

"Then say it. Tell me."

"I love you."

"Say it's a beautiful night and you're beautiful."

"It's a beautiful night and you're beautiful and I love you."

"Warm night, too."

"Yes."

"But the river is cold. Even on warm nights it's very cold."

"I know."

"I'm cold," she said.

"Not for long."

"Wet-cold, and I want to be warm."

"I'll make you warm, Janine. I will."

"Promise?"

"I promise."

She moved closer. "Kiss me."

He kissed her. Butter mouth. Soft. The feel and taste of her made him ache inside and out.

"Touch me. Here."

He touched her.

"And here."

"Oh, yes."

"Take off my suit."

His fingers trembled. She had to help him. White alabaster in the moonlight.

"Now you. All your clothes."

Again she helped him. And when he was naked, she moved into his arms. Entwining him. Touching him with electric fingers.

"So big," she said.

"Yes."

"So hard."

"Yes."

"All for me?"

"Yes!"

Her arms tightened around him. He pressed her back into the grass, stroked her, kissed her nipples, her mouth, tasted her tongue, her tongue—

"Love me," she whispered.

"Yes."

"Make me warm."

"Yes."

"Hurry, hurry! Make me warm!"

Easing into the wet hollow of her. Deep. Soft moans, hers and his both. Slow movements, faster, too fast—slowing to make it last.

"Don't wait, hurry!"

Fast again, fast, faster, fastfastfast—

Long moments of ecstasy.

But only for him.

"I'm still cold," she said.

The feathery night wind was warm on his skin, but it did nothing to take the chill from hers. She was like ice covered with goosebumps. He held her tightly, still trying to infuse her body with the heat from his own.

"Janine, I'm sorry, I'm so sorry."

"You promised you'd make me warm again."

"I tried, I won't stop trying . . ."

"Why?" she said.

He stiffened, drew back from her.

"Why?"

"You always ask me that. Don't."

"Why?"

"Please, Janine, please don't keep asking me that."

"Why?"

"I don't *know* why, I don't know."

"You don't love me. You never loved me."

"I do. I swear I do, I love you."

"I don't believe you."

"Would I have asked you to marry me if I didn't love you?"

"You didn't mean it."

"I did! I'd marry you tonight, right now— "

"It's too late."

"Don't say that. I know you still love me."

"Do I?"

"You're here, you keep coming here . . ."

"Too late."

"Keep letting me make love to you."

"Too late, too late."

"Stop saying that!"

"What will you do if I don't stop?"

"Oh God, Janine . . ."

"You're so big, so strong. What will you do?"

"Nothing, nothing . . .you have to believe that I'm sorry!"

She sat up. "Why?" she said.

"No, don't."

"Why?"

"Please!"

"Why?"

"I don't know I don't know I'm sorry I don't know!"

"Look at me," she said.

A chill swept over him, through him, made him as icy as she was. His hands began to shake. "No," he said. "Look at me."

"I can't, I won't, not again . . ."

"Look. Look. Take a close look at me."

He looked because he had to, he had no choice. He saw her face, her body change. White alabaster dissolving, layers peeling away slowly, then quickly, until bone showed beneath the nibbled strips of flesh. Both eyes vanished, leaving empty skeletal sockets that dripped water, mud, furry green moss. Something crawled out of her mouth, something like a huge swollen tongue, purple and black in the talcumy moonlight. He screamed.

She made a different sound, a choking sound. He covered his face, and moaned, and then wept.

When he lifted his head, she was Janine again. White alabaster covered by the black bathing suit, smiling her special smile over her shoulder—young and beautiful like a water sprite. Walking away. Leaving him again.

"No! Janine, don't go!"

"It's time," she said. "I can't stay any longer tonight."

Down the slope. Into the river. Not swimming this time, just walking slow and then slowly sinking. The water closed over her head, but he could still see her as if he were there with her, drifting down into the mud, the tangle of reeds, the darkness. Gone. As if she'd never been here at all.

Until the next time.

The surface smoothed, reformed into black glass. He kept on sitting there, naked, in the soft grass, soft warm breeze. Shivering. Crying.

The night, the river.

And the girl he loved. The girl he'd strangled when she first told him it was time for her to go away. The cold dead girl who kept coming back to beg him to make her warm again, and to ask him why.

All that was left of Janine.

CAT CAY

Dear Blanche,
    Well, here we are at Cat Bay on Cat Cay. Finally!
    Three different planes, the last one a twelve-seater, and
then a forty-five-minute trip by ferry launch, and *then* Arthur had
to rent a car and drive us all the way around this primitive little
island to get to Tweed's Resort. Talk about remote. I was afraid it
couldn't possibly be worth all that trouble. But it *is,* Blanche. This
isn't just another Caribbean island—it's a vacation paradise!
    Cat Bay on Cat Cay. Isn't that wonderfully alliterative? And
wonderfully descriptive too. Did I show you the brochure before
we left? I can't remember if I did or not. Anyway, the island is one
of the outer Leewards, twenty miles long and fifteen miles wide,
and from the air it really does look like a sleeping cat. There's a
long, narrow, curving peninsula at the south end shaped exactly
like a tail, and at the north end there's a rounded projection that
resembles a head and two wedge-shaped promontories, one on
either side of the head, that are perfectly symmetrical. The natives
call the promontories East Ear and West Ear. Isn't that cute?
They're the highest points on the cay—about one hundred fifty
feet above a rocky shoreline. The rest of the island is at sea level.
    Cat Bay curves in from East Ear, a mile-long sweep of bril-
liantly clear water and the most dazzling white coral sand beach.
The photos in the brochure don't do justice to it. Wait until you
see the ones I took. Tweed's Resort is at the south end, and it's
just the most marvelous mix of provincial and retro-modern. Large
bungalows with terraces practically hanging over the beach, and a
huge main house where meals and drinks are served that you'd
swear was lifted right out of one of those thirties tropical movies,
like the one with Dorothy Lamour about the hurricane. I mean,
there are ceiling fans instead of air-conditioning! And the grounds
are fabulous. Most of Cat Cay is flat and treeless, with a lot of un-
attractive scrub growth, but at Tweed's there are palms and flam-
boyant trees and frangipani and . . . oh, every kind of exotic plant

you can imagine. And old stone fences and rusty cannons from the days of the Spanish Main pirates, when Captain Kidd, Blackbeard, and Anne Bonny and Calico Jack Rackam (whoever *they* were) came all the way out here to pillage and plunder. The whole place simply *drips* atmosphere.

The owner, Jeremiah Tweed, is a delightful old graybeard, the last member of an African slave family that first settled here two or three hundred years ago. He speaks a charming native patois and tells the most breathtaking stories. His wife, Vera, does most of the cooking and is an absolute wizard—the meal we had last night was to die for. Crayfish, curried conch, and a barbecued meat they claim is beef but Arthur and I are convinced is *goat.* Not that I really want to know, Blanche, because it's delicious no matter what kind of animal it came from.

And here's the big surprise, not mentioned at all in the brochure: the place is positively teeming with cats! Dozens and dozens, nearly every variety of mixed-breed shorthair and longhair, and most as friendly as can be. Mr. Tweed says he and his wife are lifelong cat fanciers and maybe they are, or maybe they feed them and let them roam free as a promotional ploy because of Cat Bay on Cat Cay, but in any case *I* certainly approve. You know how I love cats. Of course, Arthur started grumbling as soon as he saw how many there are. He never has been able to warm up to felines, at least not the non-feral, four-footed kind.

We practically have the resort to ourselves, since the season is still a few weeks off. That would suit me just fine if it wasn't for the Tweeds' only other guest. Her name is Gloria Bartell and she's a widow from Chicago. *Claims* to be a widow, at any rate. She can't be more than thirty-five, one of those slinky blondes with ball-bearing hips and a Lauren Bacall voice. As soon as I laid eyes on her I said to myself, uh-oh, here's a woman on the make. Arthur doesn't think so, naturally. He says she's just a lonely widow with no designs on anything except crayfish and rum punches. But he doesn't fool me. I caught him ogling her in her skimpy bikini this morning, when we came out to the beach. She was lying under one of the little palm-frond lean-tos they have scattered around for shade, and without even asking me he sat down under the one closest to her. And then started a conversation that all but excluded me. Believe you me, I told him what I thought of *that* behavior when we were alone afterward.

Anyhow, Blanche, I'm not going to let myself worry about the widow or anything else. I'm here to have fun. Cuddle with Arthur, swim, go sailing, lie in the sun as much as I can stand to so I'll come home with a glorious tan that will make you green with envy, even if it is on a pudgy forty-three-year-old body. I'm not going to worry about my weight, either, not with all those scrumptious Caribbean specialties of Mrs. Tweed's and Mr. Tweed's special rum punches.

I'll write again in a day or two, whenever the mood strikes. Meanwhile, take care and be sure to let me know if and when that handsome tennis pro at the club says yes next time you ask him for a private lesson. If I wasn't a hopelessly old-fashioned, one-man woman, I'd be terribly jealous of you.

Love and kisses,

Janice

October 23

Dear Blanche,

Greetings again from beautiful Cat Bay on Cat Cay.

We went snorkeling yesterday, all the way out to the coral reef that protects the bay from sharks (the kind that live in the ocean, anyhow). The water is only about six feet deep the whole way, and so clear it's like looking down through layers of glass; you can see starfish and anemones and all sorts of other sea creatures. I worked on my tan most of the afternoon, until clouds piled up and it rained for a while. This morning I went for a lovely catamaran ride around to West Ear. Arthur didn't go along. He said he just wanted to lie on the beach and read and I couldn't talk him out of it.

Do I sound less enthusiastic than I did two days ago, Blanche? If I do, it's because I am. I'm not having near as good a time as I thought I would. You know I planned this trip as more than just a vacation, as a second honeymoon for Arthur and me. But it isn't working out that way. We don't seem to be communicating—not in *any* way, if you know what I mean. Our bungalow has two double beds and we haven't shared the same one for even a minute since we arrived.

I blame Arthur, of course. And that Bartell woman I told you about in my last letter. She hardly has a civil word for me, but she flirts shamelessly with him. He preens when she does it, too—not that I have to tell you about that annoying habit of his when he's around an attractive female.

Last night he went for a walk after dinner, without asking me to join him, and a little while later I happened to step out onto the terrace and there they were, Arthur and the widow, walking along the beach side by side, talking and laughing. One of the Tweeds' cats came bounding out of the bushes just then and ran toward them. Just being playful, the way cats are. And Arthur picked up a piece of driftwood and threw it at the poor little thing. I think he hit it, too, because I heard it cry before it ran off. Then they both laughed as if they'd shared a wonderful joke. I mean, have you ever heard of anything so cruel and heartless?

Then today, after I returned from the catamaran trip, there they were together again, in the garden at the main house, drinking rum punches with their heads about six inches apart. A few minutes ago, when we got back to our bungalow, I confronted Arthur point-blank and of course he laughed it off. All perfectly innocent, my dear—*he* says. Well, we'll see.

So that's why I'm not my usual cheery self today. I know you understand, Blanche, and I wish you were here so we could talk about it. You're the only person I can really talk to—my one true friend. More later. Until then,

Love and kisses,
Janice

October 24

Dear Blanche,

Last night after dinner Arthur left on another of his walks. I tried to join him, but he wouldn't hear of it. Well, I waited fifteen minutes and then I went down to Gloria Bartell's bungalow. The lights were on inside, but when I crept onto the terrace and peeked through the jalousies, she wasn't there. I went straight to the beach. It was a beautiful moonlit night—one of those magnificent frosty white Caribbean moons that make everything seem as bright as day—and I could see all the way to East Ear. There was no sign of either of them. And no sign of them at the main house or anywhere else on the grounds.

It was more than two hours before Arthur came back. I asked him where he'd been, and he said walking on the beach, enjoying the moonlight and the peace and quiet.

Oh, Blanche, it looks like he's at it again. I don't want to believe it after he swore to me the last time that he'd never again be unfaithful. I keep hoping I'm wrong, imagining things. But under the circumstances, what else *can* I believe?

Your troubled friend,
Janice

October 25

Dear Blanche,

I wasn't wrong. It's all true.

Arthur *is* having a clandestine affair with that Bartell witch. And he doesn't even care that I know it!

He disappeared this afternoon for four and a half hours. And so did she. And when he came back . . . well, one look at him and his clothes and it was painfully obvious to anyone with half a brain what he'd been doing for most of the time he was gone. I came right out and accused him of it, naturally. He didn't even bother to deny it. All he said was, "What I do is my business, Janice. I'm tired of answering to you. In fact I'm tired of *you* and of pretending I'm not just because you control the damn purse strings."

I cried my eyes out afterward. Then I swallowed the last of my pride and went to him and begged and pleaded—and he laughed at me. Exactly the way he laughed after he hit that poor little cat with the piece of driftwood. As if I were nothing to him anymore—if I ever was in the first place—except a cruel joke.

Oh, Blanche, what am I going to do?

Desperately,

Janice

October 27

Dear Blanche,

I just tried to call you. But the telephone system on Cat Cay is so hopelessly antiquated I couldn't get through. At least the Tweeds have a fax machine, one of their few concessions to modern technology. Otherwise I wouldn't be able to let you know this quickly what's happened.

Blanche, I have some ghastly news.

Arthur is dead!

It happened last night, around ten-thirty. He hardly said a word to me all day, and after supper he left me alone again and went to meet *her,* and he didn't come back. I thought. . . well, I thought he'd given up on our marriage completely and didn't care about keeping up appearances and had spent the night in her bungalow. I didn't go to check because I couldn't bear to know for sure. I just lay awake the entire night, waiting for him and crying hopelessly.

When dawn came I couldn't stand it any longer. I *had* to confront him and get it over with. So I got dressed and went to the witch's bungalow. Well, she was there alone and she claimed Arthur hadn't spent the night with her, that she hadn't seen him since nine-thirty last night. Oh, they'd been together then, she admitted that, but only for a walk over to the bottom of East Ear. He wanted to climb up onto the promontory to take in the view, she said, but she didn't because there are signs warning you the footing is treacherous and not to make the climb after dark. So she left him there and walked back alone.

I was frightened that something had happened to him and she acted as if she was too. We both ran to the main house and told Mr. Tweed, and he and two of his employees hurried out to East Ear and that was where they found Arthur. Not up on the Ear but among the jagged rocks at its base. He fell more than a hundred feet, Mr. Tweed said. He must have been a horrible sight, too, because I wasn't allowed to go and look at the body.

Everything since has just been a blur. The local police constable, a nice little man named Kitts, drove out from the village and asked a lot of questions. Then he and his men left to transport Arthur's remains to the village hospital. He'll be back later to "attend to formalities," as he put it.

When he does I'm going to tell him about the witch coming on to Arthur, trying to seduce him. But not that she actually succeeded, because I don't *know* that she did and because there's no reason to open up that can of worms unless it's absolutely necessary. Why say anything at all, you're wondering? Well, everybody seems to think Arthur's death was an accident, but was it, Blanche? I mean, for all I know the witch went up onto East Ear with him after all and they had some kind of argument and she *pushed* him over the edge. And if that's the way it happened, then I want her to get what's coming to her too.

More about that later. I'd better fax this right now, before the constable returns and while I still have my wits about me.

In deepest despair,

Janice

October 28

Dear Blanche,

Thank you so much, my dear friend, for the heartwarming words of solace and sympathy. You've always been there for me in my hour of need, and never more selflessly than now. I can't tell you how much it means to me.

No, you mustn't even think of flying all the way out here. By the time you arrived I'd be on my way home. Constable Kitts says I can leave tomorrow and I've already arranged to take the most direct route possible. I'm sure I can hold up well enough until I get there, and once I see you I'll let myself go and we'll have a good long cry together.

I'm sorry I wasn't able to fax this reply to you yesterday, but your fax arrived just after the constable's return. And after that, the rest of the day simply melted away for me and I was exhausted by nightfall. Constable Kitts and his "formalities," which translated into more questions and all sorts of papers to sign. Mr. and Mrs. Tweed fussing around, trying to console me. Even the witch tried to offer her sympathy, but of course I wouldn't let her anywhere near me. The sheer gall of the woman!

But evidently she's not a murderess. At least the constable doesn't think so. For one thing, she did leave Arthur when she said she did and walk back from East Ear alone. She stopped at the main house for a nightcap, and the Tweeds both remember that it was just ten when she got there. And Arthur's watch was broken in the fall and the hands were frozen at 10:34. So the official verdict is that his death was a tragic accident, which I suppose, when one takes the long view, will be much easier on me. Constable Kitts thinks one of two things must have happened. Either Arthur lost his footing on the rough ground, or he tripped over one of the Tweeds' cats—a more likely occurrence than you might think because many of them go wandering up there at night to hunt birds and rodents. Wouldn't it be ironic if he *did* trip over one of the cats, considering how he felt about them and his inexcusable cruelty on the beach the other day?

The witch has left Cat Bay and temporarily moved into a hotel in the village. Constable Kitts is letting her leave the island tomorrow too, and good riddance, even if she didn't get what was coming to her. I'm still here at the resort, though in a different bungalow than the one I shared with Arthur. The Tweeds have been marvelous, bringing me food and drinks and hovering around to see if there's anything else I need. A cynic might say they're worried that I'll sue them for negligence or something and that's why they're being so solicitous. But I'm not a cynic, Blanche, you know that. I'm just a poor, unlucky woman who seems fated to lead a tragically unfulfilled life.

No, no, don't worry, I'm not *that* depressed. I'll survive this setback and press on. Always have, always will.

One thing that is keeping me from becoming too self-pitying is that I have a part-time roommate in my new bungalow—the cutest little calico with one orange paw and the longest whiskers you've ever seen. She follows me around and coaxes me at every opportunity into picking her up and cuddling her. It's as if she understands and sympathizes with me and is determined to give me comfort. Isn't it a shame that all people aren't as sweet-natured as most cats? Men particularly.

Husbands definitely.

I didn't tell Constable Kitts about Roy and George, of course. It's really nobody's business but mine—and yours, dear Blanche—that Arthur was my third husband and the third to die in a terrible accident. Coincidences do happen, after all, and everyone knows that tragedies come in threes. It's not my fault I keep falling in love with men who turn out to be faithless fortune hunters *and* prone to fatal accidents.

I mean, you and I both know I'm not only a poor and unlucky woman, but a helpless one. Don't we, Blanche?

Love and kisses,

Janice

ALL THE SAME

J EFFORDS LAY on the bed, smoking and thinking about Penny. Outside the open window, the night was choked with heat. The air smelled of mesquite; there was no moon. He listened to the night sounds. An animal screamed somewhere in the desert, and in the motel courtyard, a car engine idled roughly. Voices rose from the room next door, shrill, plaintive.

The cigarette was raw in Jeffords' throat. He stubbed it out in the glass ashtray resting on his bare chest. He wore only a pair of shorts, and sweat coated his skin, glistening in the darkness. The sheets were wet beneath him.

"You fool!" somebody said clearly in the next room, and then it was silent again.

Jeffords reached across to the night stand for another cigarette; the pack was empty. He tried to remember if there was a machine in the motel office. Potted plant and wrought iron furniture and a long, flat Formica counter; rack with magazines . . . Was there a damned machine in that office?

His temples had begun to throb. Jeffords swung his legs off the bed and sat with his head in his hands. After a time he got to his feet, located a towel under his clothes on the chair, and wiped his chest dry. Then he put on his trousers and a soiled white shirt, not buttoning the shirt, and opened the door and stepped outside.

The motel was set in the shape of a horseshoe, with the open end facing out toward the highway. The office was the first one on the right as you came in. His room was at the closed end of the horseshoe.

Jeffords stood there breathing the thick air through his mouth. There was a white stone patio in the center of the courtyard, with an oval-shaped swimming pool, a strobe light mounted behind it, at one end. The light flashed red and blue and green, and the glare hurt Jeffords' eyes after the darkness of the room.

The drive that circled the patio was graveled; his steps crunched loudly in the stillness as he walked toward the office. A small white light burned over the door. As he approached, Jeffords could see a sleek white sports car parked in the driveway beside the office; its engine was idling, and Jeffords thought that it must be the one he had heard from his room. Someone was behind the wheel, a black, still shadow.

Jeffords passed the car and came up to the office. Just as he did, the door opened and a girl came out. He stopped. She was blonde, with her hair pulled into a ponytail at the back, fastened with a wide blue band. She wore a pair of white shorts and a yellow bolero-type shirt with little bobbing tassels on the bottom.

She cocked her head to one side, holding the office door open with one hand, looking at him. A quizzical smile played at the corners of her mouth. Jeffords wanted to say something to her, but he could not think of anything. He wet his lips and nodded meaninglessly. She was still holding the door; he reached out and took it, and she gave him a wide smile and then went to where the car stood idling.

Jeffords watched her get inside. The black shadow at the wheel let out the clutch. The rear tires spun, spewing gravel. The car went to the closed end of the horseshoe and stopped before a room two away from Jeffords'. He realized he was still holding the door open. He turned and went inside.

The fat woman in the shapeless sundress who had given him the room that afternoon was still behind the counter. She was looking at Jeffords as he came in. "Yeah?" she said.

"You have a cigarette machine?" he asked.

"Right there against the wall."

Jeffords went to the machine, seeing himself in the mirrored front. His black hair was tangled and damp and beard stubble flecked his gaunt cheeks. His deep-set eyes were rimmed in red. He fished in his pocket for change; all he had was a quarter. He took out his wallet and went to the counter again.

"Change for a dollar?"

"No change," the woman said.

"What do you mean, no change?"

"Just that. Safe's locked for the night."

"Then open it," Jeffords said irritably. "I want to get some cigarettes."

"Can't."

"Well, why the hell not?"

"Watch your mouth, sonny."

"Listen," Jeffords said, "how can you run a damned business? Suppose somebody comes in for a room?"

"I said to watch your mouth," the woman told him. She had little pig eyes and they were staring a hole through Jeffords.

"You fat old biddy," he said.

The woman's face grew bright red. She stood up, pointed a finger; fat jiggled on her bare arm like gelatin. "I'll have you thrown out, you bum!" she shouted. "You get out of here or I'll have my husband throw you out!"

Jeffords stared at her. "You're all the same," he said. "Every one of you."

"What? What?"

He turned and went outside and slammed the door.

Back in his room, he lay once more on the bed. Immediately, he began to think about Penny—his wife Penny. Damn her, why had she run out on him the way she had? What had made her take up with that big, ugly salesman? He'd given her everything, bought her fine clothes, and still she'd run off with that salesman after just three months of marriage. She'd taken all the money with her, too—almost four thousand dollars from their joint checking and savings accounts; all she'd left him was the six hundred dollars in his special account, the six hundred which had dwindled to the four hundred and eighty he now had in his wallet.

Six hundred dollars and the furnished apartment and his car, that was all.

When he'd discovered that she was gone, he'd been half-crazy. He hadn't known what to do. Finally, he had quit his job and packed his few belongings in his car and gone looking for her. That had been ten days ago, and now here he was, in the middle of the desert, with no idea where to go next. Where was there to go? A hundred places, a thousand places, and all of them empty . . .

Jeffords lay looking up at the ceiling. He had slept very little in the past week, and it was beginning to tell on him; he dozed, lying there. The sharp knocking on the door snapped him off the bed and onto his feet, his heart pounding wildly, his head spinning with the fog of sleep.

The knocking grew more insistent.

Jeffords put on his trousers and went to the door, shaking his head and wiping sweat and sleep from his eyes. It was the girl from the sports car, the blonde girl with the ponytail. Her eyes were wide and dark and flashing, and the front of her bolero shirt was torn.

"Let me in, will you?" she said.

Jeffords did not know what to think. "What is it?"

"Just let me in," the girl said. "Please let me in."

"All right." He stood aside and she came in and he shut the door behind her.

"He tried to attack me," she said, turning to look at him.

"Who did?"

"Van."

"Who's Van?"

"The fellow I was with," the girl said. "I had to hit him. I hit him with a lamp."

Jeffords felt a sudden panic. "Listen, I don't want to get involved in anything."

"I knocked him out," the girl said. "He's lying in my room, knocked out."

"Why did you come to me? What do you want me to do?"

"I don't know. I remembered you from the office."

"How did you know which room was mine?"

"I saw you through the window when you came back."

Jeffords sat down on the bed. "Why did you come here with this Van? Didn't you know he'd try something?"

"No, he was nice and polite when he gave me the ride," the girl said. "When he suggested we stop for the night, he said we'd take separate rooms and he even let me go in to register. I said good night to him but a little while later he forced his way into my room and went kind of wild." She paused, studying Jeffords. "Look, are you waiting here or something? For somebody to come?"

"No," he said.

"When are you leaving?"

"In the morning."

"Can't you go now?"

"What for?"

"I want to get away from here. Can you take me with you?"

"You're nuts," Jeffords said. "I can't take you."

"Have you got a wife somewhere?"

"No," Jeffords said bitterly. "I don't have any wife."

"Where are you going?"

"I don't know. Los Angeles, maybe."

"Take me along."

"I can't do that."

"I don't want to be here when Van wakes up," the girl said. "I don't know what he might do."

"I can't help you."

"And I don't like the police. We don't get along too well, the police and me."

"I'm sorry."

"Come on," she said. "Please."

Jeffords stared at her, at her pleading eyes, and he felt himself softening inside. Girls like her—like Penny—always affected him that way. He wanted to believe in them, in their basic goodness, and he always ended up getting involved in one way or another.

He moistened his lips. *You're crazy if you do it,* he told himself. *She's trouble. Can't you see it? She's just like Penny; she's another one of the same. Don't do it, don't get involved with her.*

Even as he thought this, he heard himself saying, "All right, come on," as if his vocal chords and his brain were separate entities, as if he were two people instead of one.

"Thanks," she said breathlessly. "Thanks."

Jeffords had just one suitcase, and he threw his clothes into it and put on his shirt. The girl took his arm and they went outside.

He said, "Do you have any luggage?"

"Just one small bag."

"You'd better get it."

"I don't want to go back over there."

"I'll go with you. You don't want to leave your stuff here."

"What if Van's conscious by now? I didn't hit him very hard."

"If he is, I'll take care of him."

They went across to the girl's unit and inside. Van was a pudgy man in his late forties, lying face down with his arms spread. There was blood on his right temple, but he was breathing. The porcelain lamp the girl had hit him with was shattered on the floor beside him.

"Is he still out?" she asked.

"Yeah."

She gathered up her bag and they went outside again. She said, "Where's your car?"

"Over there."

"Let's go then, before he wakes up."

Jeffords felt the hot desert wind on his face, blowing in through the open window. He stared out at the long, straight black ribbon of the highway. The desert was a half-world of shadows on either side.

The girl—her name was Marcy, she told him—leaned against the passenger door, watching him. After a while she said, "You're kind of quiet, aren't you?"

"Sometimes."

She laughed. "You have to watch out for the quiet ones."

Jeffords was silent for a moment. Then he said, "What are you doing out here? All by yourself?"

"Just drifting with the wind," Marcy said. "Hitchhiking. Seeing some of this big wide country."

"You're kind of young for that."

"Oh, hell."

"You can get into a lot of trouble."

"Like with Van, you mean?"

"Like with him."

"There aren't many like him."

"How old are you, anyway?"

"Twenty-one."

"You ought to be married or something," Jeffords said, and wondered why he had said it.

Marcy laughed. "Sure, someday. Right now, my bag is grins. That's what makes the world go round."

Like Penny, he thought. *Just like Penny. Why did I have to take her with me, why did I have to feel sorry for her?*

"Hey," Marcy said, "have you ever been to Los Angeles?"

"Yes," Jeffords answered.

"It must be some place. Everybody I ever knew who went to Los Angeles said it was some place."

"It's some place, all right."

Marcy yawned and turned on the seat, moving close to Jeffords. She put her head on his shoulder. "I'm getting sleepy," she said.

"Go to sleep then."

"Okay. You don't mind?"

"No, I don't mind."

They drove through the night and, subtly, Jeffords felt his mood change. He could smell the soft, sweet fragrance of the girl's hair, and her body was warm resting against his. *She's just a kid,* he thought. *Kind of wild, but nice—a good kid. Maybe she's different from the rest, maybe she's one of the good ones . . .*

It was past dawn when Marcy awoke. They were coming out of the desert now, into Barstow. The morning sun was hot, bright, in the eastern sky; the reflection of it off the shining metal of the hood was blinding, but it didn't bother Jeffords, not at all.

Marcy stretched. "Where are we?"

"Barstow. How did you sleep?"

"Like the proverbial log."

"Are you hungry?"

"Am I!"

"We'll stop for breakfast."

They ate bacon and eggs at a small cafe, and Jeffords found himself in a light, carefree mood. It was the girl who made him feel that way. He couldn't explain it; it was almost as if he were coming alive again, as if things mattered again. *Marcy*, he thought, savoring the name. *Marcy*.

They lingered over coffee, bought sandwiches for the remainder of the trip. They drove through to the coast, stopping once to eat a picnic lunch. They laughed a lot, talked a lot, and Jeffords' buoyant mood increased. By the time they reached Los Angeles, shortly after dark, he felt as he had on his honeymoon with Penny: right with everything, happy with everything.

"Well," he said, "we made it."

"We made it, all right."

"Do you want to stop somewhere?"

"Okay. You must be tired."

"I am."

They took a motel—two rooms with a connecting door between. Marcy kissed him good night with feeling and promise, and he went to bed and slept deeply, dreaming good dreams.

He awoke at ten in the morning, rested. He got up and dressed and opened the connecting door, peered into the adjoining room.

Marcy wasn't there.

Jeffords went outside and looked around and didn't see her. He walked down to the motel office. The same man who had given them the rooms the night before was still there.

"Have you seen the girl I came here with?" Jeffords asked.

"Oh, I saw her, sure," the man said.

"Where is she?"

"Gone."

"Gone? Gone where?"

The man shrugged. "She got on the San Diego bus."

"What? She got on the what?"

"The bus for San Diego," the man said. "It stops right out front. She got on about an hour ago. I figured the two of you—"

Jeffords did not hear the rest of it. He ran outside and back to his room. His temples were pounding as he opened his suitcase; he had put his wallet in there the night before, when he had gone to bed. The wallet was still there, spread open on top of his shirts. He picked it up.

It was empty.

Jeffords stood remembering the pudgy man, Van, lying on the floor of the motel unit in the desert. Marcy had said he'd tried to attack her, but maybe the truth was, he had caught her going through his things, looking for money or valuables. Or maybe the truth was, she hadn't wanted to wait for him to go to sleep—she had hit him with the lamp when his back was turned. Well, it didn't matter. Nothing mattered now.

Jeffords put his wallet back into the suitcase. He took the car keys from his pocket, went outside to where his car was parked and opened the trunk. There was a small brown box inside, behind the spare tire, and he took that out and returned to the motel room.

He put the case on the writing desk, unfastened the catches, and took out the gun.

He stood looking at it for a time. Then he put it into his belt, under his shirt, took the suitcase and the small box out to his car, and left the motel. He drove onto the freeway, south toward San Diego.

They're all the same, he thought. *All the same, every one of them in the world.*

He knew what he had to do.

When he found Marcy, he would put the muzzle of the gun against her heart and he would pull the trigger—just like he had done with Penny when he'd found her alone in the Las Vegas motel three days before . . .

PRIVATE TERRORS

IT WAS ONE of those pointless arguments you get into sometimes with strangers in bars, diners, other public places. Pointless because nobody ever changes anybody else's opinion. Politics, religion, sports—the topic doesn't really matter. This time it happened to be horror flicks.

The tavern was a little hole-in-the-wall near Golden Gate Park. I'd never been there before, but I was in the neighborhood and it was a cold, blustery night and I needed something to warm me up before I ate. Two people in the place, even though it was only about nine o'clock—a bald-headed bartender and a little guy down at the far corner of the bar nuzzling a glass of something that glinted dark red in the backbar lights.

Some nights you feel like company and some nights you don't. This was a company night, so I picked out a stool two removed from where the little guy was parked, at right angles to him. He looked up at me, cocking his head to one side. Geezer, I saw then. At least seventy, with a shriveled-gourd face and hair as fuzzy-thin and white as an Angora cat's. His eyes were bright and sharp, though. They held on mine in a way that said he wouldn't mind some company himself.

"Cold night," I said. "Must be in the forties out there."

"Yes."

"I'm on my way home from work. What brings you out on a night like this?"

"I have been to the cinema," he said.

Cinema. He didn't speak with an accent, but his English was too precise to be natural to him. Foreign-born, probably, emigrated to this country at a young age. Naturalized citizen now. That's a game I play when I meet somebody for the first time—try to figure out something about them from the way they look and talk and act.

The bartender came down and I ordered Wild Turkey neat. "Pour one for yourself," I said then.

"Can't do it," he said. He patted his paunch. "Ulcer."

I looked at the old guy. "How about you? Another of whatever you're having?"

"Yes, thank you. The same, please, George."

"One Turkey neat, one port. Coming up."

"So you've been to the movies," I said to the old guy, making conversation. "What'd you see?"

"There is a theater nearby that shows classic films."

"Is that so? What was on tonight?"

"Dracula."

"The '31 original with Lugosi?"

"Yes, but it is not the true original, only the first spoken film version."

"Right," I said. "The first vampire flick was a silent, made in Germany around 1920."

"1922," the old guy said. *"Nosferatu, eine Symphonie des Grauens.* The role of Count Orlok was played by Max Schrek. It is the earliest surviving screen version depicting Dracula, but it is not the first vampire film."

"No?"

"Four others preceded it, all produced in this country and all with similar titles." He ticked them off on his fingers. *"The Vampire,* based on the Kipling poem, in 1910. *The Vampire* in 1915. *Vampire Ambrose* in 1916. *Vampire* in 1920."

"Probably all lost now," I said.

"Two are not lost. I have copies."

"No kidding? I didn't know any of those obscure silents were available on VHS or DVD."

"They are not."

"You don't mean you have original sixteen-millimeter prints?"

"Yes."

"Wow," I said, impressed. "Must have taken some doing to track them down."

"It was very difficult, yes."

"I wouldn't mind seeing them. You also have *Nosferatu?*"

"Yes."

"I'd really like to see that one."

It was as much a feeler question as a comment, but he just let it lie there without picking it up. Okay, so no invitation.

"So happens I'm a horror movie fan myself," I said. "Collect anything in the genre I can put my hands on. I must have a couple of dozen vampire flicks, but I prefer the later ones, you know? Vincent Price in *The Last Man on Earth.* Christopher Lee as the

Prince of Darkness in the '58 Hammer production of *Dracula.* Coppola's '92 version with Gary Oldman. *Blade, Queen of the Damned*—"

The old guy's mouth had quirked up as if he wanted to spit. "Trash," he said.

"What's that?"

"Trash. Modern films do not stimulate the mind, they assault the senses."

"You consider movies made in the 50s and 60s modern?"

"I do."

"Oh, I get it. You're one of these guys who dislikes color. Everything in your collection is black and white or grainy sepia, right?"

"There is far greater subtlety and nuance in films of black and white," he said stiffly. "But it is not color that I dislike."

"What, then?"

"Barbarism. Visual obscenities."

"You mean in-your-face violence?"

"I do not care to view torn flesh and fountains of blood."

The bartender had brought our drinks and was standing off a little way, listening or trying not to listen. I treated myself to a long pull of Wild Turkey; the old guy took a small, delicate sip from the glass of port he'd been nursing.

I said, "So what else do you collect besides bloodless black and white vampire flicks?"

"Nothing else."

"That's all? What about werewolves? The Frankenstein monster? Mummies and Egyptian curses?"

"The only truly frightening creature of legend is the vampire."

Something to do with where he was born, I thought. Hungary, Croatia, Transylvania—one of those places where the vampire legend was deeply ingrained in the culture.

"Maybe, if you say so. But there are a lot of other pretty horrific things on and off celluloid."

"Perhaps," he said.

"Not perhaps—definitely. Hellspawn beings, for instance. The demon in *Curse of the Demon.* Damian, *Rosemary's Baby.*"

Quick dismissive flip of his hand.

"Witches and warlocks. *Burn, Witch, Burn, The Devil's Own, The Blair Witch Project.*"

Flip.

"Ghosts and other supernatural creatures," I said. He was start-ing to annoy me. *"The Uninvited, The Haunting of Hill House, Ghost Story."*

Flip.

"The Grim Reaper. *Donovan's Brain, The Man Who Could Cheat Death.* Or one of Poe's death obsessions—*The Premature Burial, Masque of the Red Death, The Tell-Tale Heart."*

"Such things do not interest or disturb me," he said.

"You're one of the few then. How about giant beasts? King Kong, the Abominable Snowman, Bigfoot, Godzilla. Monster snakes and spiders and crabs and insects. Kronos. The Fifty-Foot Woman."

"Childish nonsense."

Now I was really annoyed. "You could say the same about vampires."

He pursed his lips and peered again into the dark red depths of his port.

"Okay, then. Other kinds of mutants. *The Creature from the Black Lagoon, The Toxic Avenger*, the voodoo zombies in *I Walked With a Zombie* and the flesh eaters in *Night of the Living Dead."*

Flip.

I said between my teeth, "Beings from another planet. You must've seen the original black and white *Invasion of the Body Snatchers."*

"Yes."

"And?"

"It did not frighten me."

"What about *Alien*? That one scared the hell out of me."

"I have not seen it."

"Well, that's no big surprise. Too recent, too bloody, too color."

He gave me a long, unreadable look. "Tell me, young man. What is it that truly frightens you? What is your private terror?"

"My what?"

"Every person has one thing that terrifies him more than any other. What is yours? Alien beings from another world?"

"Not hardly."

"Ghosts, demons, mutant creatures?"

"No. You want to know what kind of flick scares me the most, pop? All right, I'll tell you. The ones where the monsters are hu-man."

"Yes?"

"That's right. Ordinary on the surface, depraved underneath—the type that commits wholesale slaughter for no reason except homicidal compulsion or the sheer joy of it. They're the most terrifying thing there is."

No comment. But no flip, either.

"Norman Bates in *Psycho*, there's one example," I said. "You ever see *Psycho*?"

"Once, long ago. It did not move me."

"Well, it moved *me*. Damn near gave me a bowel movement the first time I saw that shower scene." I swallowed some more sour mash. "Jack the Ripper, Norman Bates, Freddy Krueger, Michael Myers, Hannibal Lector—they're the riders in my nightmares."

"Yet you own films about such human monsters. View them when you are alone."

"Damn right."

"Why?"

"For the same reason you collect and watch old vampire movies," I said. "You're terrified of those phantom bloodsuckers, a deep-down, gut-churning, irrational fear, and the only way you can justify it to yourself is to take the scholarly approach—subtlety, nuance, all that shit. That's the coward's way of dealing with it. That's why you don't like to see blood—it makes your fear too real, too intense. Just the opposite with me. I deal with my private terror by wallowing in it, letting it assault my senses, feeling what the victims feel—"

The old guy shoved his stool back and stood up. He wasn't looking at me anymore; his face had a pinched, chalky look. He lifted his glass and drained it in a series of quick sips, set it down, walked around behind me and straight out of there without a word or a backward glance. The wind slammed the door shut after him.

The bartender came over. "Couldn't help overhearing," he said. "You hit him where he lives."

"Yeah. I didn't mean to be so rough on him, but he was getting under my skin."

"He had it coming. Harmless old bird, but when it comes to his favorite subject he can be a pain in the ass. Vampires, for Christ's sake."

"He can't help it," I said. "Part of his heritage. None of us can help where we were born or what we were born with."

"Guess you're right. How about another round?"

"Better not. Time to get a bite to eat before I go home. Booze always makes me hungry."

"I know what you mean," the bartender said. "There's a pretty good diner over on Irving, stays open late. Maude's Cafe."

"Thanks. Maybe I'll give it a try."

I went back to the men's room. All the talk with the old guy had whetted my appetite for horror flicks, just as the Wild Turkey had whetted it for food. While I was taking a leak I sorted through my mental catalogue of the tapes and DVDs in my collection. When I got home I'd watch *Silence of the Lambs* or *The Texas Chainsaw Massacre* or maybe *Saw*. I was in a mood tonight to indulge my private terror.

There was a rear exit near the rest rooms, so I went out that way. Narrow alley, stuffed with cold black. I pulled up the collar on my coat and started toward the faintly lit mouth at the far end.

Noise up ahead. Movement.

Somebody lurking over behind that line of garbage cans?

I stopped, keening the shadows. Nothing but the wind for a few seconds. Then I picked up more sound and movement, a clicking and scurrying.

Rat. Young one.

I measured the distance. Twenty feet, well within the limit of my reach. I caught the animal with a quick flick of my second tongue, expanded my mouth, snapped the rat back inside, razor-toothed it in half, and ate it in two bites.

Good. Warm and spicy.

I moved on through the windy dark, out of the alley and over toward Golden Gate Park. Even on a night like this there'd be plenty of game around.

The rat had been tasty, but not much more than a snack.

I was still hungry.

ONE NIGHT AT DOLORES PARK

(A "Nameless Detective" story)

D OLORES PARK used to be the hub of one of the better
residential neighborhoods in San Francisco: acres of tall
palms and steeply rolling lawns in the Western Mission,
a gentrifying area up until a few years ago. Well-off Yuppies,
lured by sweeping views and an easy commute to downtown,
bought and renovated many of the old Victorians that rim the park.
Singles and couples, straights and gays, moved into duplexes that
sold for $300,000 and apartments that rented for upwards of a
grand a month. WASPs, Latinos, Asian Americans . . . an eclectic
mix that lived pretty much in harmony and were dedicated to pre-
serving as much of the urban good life as was left these days.

Then the drug dealers moved in.

Marijuana sellers at first, aiming their wares at students at
nearby Mission High School. The vanguard's success brought in a
scruffier variety and their equally scruffy customers. As many as
forty dealers allegedly had been doing business in Dolores Park on
recent weekends, according to published reports. The cops
couldn't do much; marijuana selling and buying is a low-priority
crime in the city. But the lack of control, the wide-open, open-air
market, brought in fresh troops: heroin and crack dealers. And
where you've got hard drugs, you also have high stakes and violence. Eight shootings and two homicides in and around Dolores
Park so far this year. The firebombing of the home of a young
couple who tried to form an activist group to fight the dealers.
Muggings, burglaries, intimidation of residents.

The result was bitterly predictable: frightened people moving
out, real-estate values dropping, and as the dealers widened their
territory to include Mission Playground down on 19th Street, the
entire neighborhood beginning to decline. The police had stepped
up patrols and were making arrests, but it was too little too late:
They didn't have the manpower or the funds, and there was so
damned much of the same thing happening elsewhere in the city.

"It's like Armageddon," one veteran cop was quoted as saying. "And the forces of evil are winning."

They were winning tonight, no question of that. It was a warm October night and I had been staked out on the west side of the park, nosed downhill near the intersection of Church and 19th, since a few minutes before six o'clock. Before it got dark I had counted seven drug transactions within the limited range of my vision—and no police presence other than a couple of cruising patrol cars. Once darkness closed down, the park had emptied fast. Now, at nine-ten, the lawns and paths appeared deserted. But I wouldn't have wanted to walk around over there, as early as it was. If there were men lurking in the shadows—and there probably were—they were dealers armed to the teeth and/or desperate junkies hunting prey. Only damned fools wandered through Dolores Park after nightfall.

Drugs, drug dealers, and the rape of a fine old neighborhood had nothing to do with why I was here; all of those things were a depressing by-product. I was here to serve a subpoena on a man named Thurmond, as a favor to a lawyer I knew. Thurmond was being sought for testimony in a huge stock-fraud case. He didn't want to testify because he was afraid of being indicted himself, and he had been hiding out as a result. It had taken me three days to find out he was holed up with an old college buddy. The college buddy owned the blue and white Stick Victorian two doors down Church Street from where I was sitting. He was home—I'd seen him arrive, and there were lights on now behind the curtained bay windows—but there was still no sign of Thurmond. I was bored as well as depressed, and irritated, and frustrated. If Thurmond gave me any trouble when he finally put in an appearance, he was going to be sorry for it.

That was what I was thinking when I saw the woman.

She came down 19th, alone, walking fast and hard. The stride and the drawn-back set of her body said she was angry about something. There was a streetlight on the corner, and when she passed under it I could see that she was thirtyish, dark-haired, slender. Wearing a light sweater over a blouse and slacks. She waited for a car to roll by—it didn't slow—and then crossed the street toward the path.

Not smart, lady, I thought. Even if she was a junkie looking to make a connection, it wasn't smart. I had been slouched down on my spine; I sat up straighter to get a better squint at where she was headed. Not into the park, at least. Away from me on the sidewalk, downhill toward Cumberland. Moving at the same hard, angry pace.

I had a fleeting impulse to chase after her, tell her to get her tail off the street. Latent paternal instinct. Hell, if she wanted to risk her safety, that was her prerogative; the world is full of what the newspeakers call "cerebrally challenged individuals." It was none of my business what happened to her—

Yes, it was.

Right then it became my business.

A line of trees and shrubs flanked the sidewalk where she was, with a separating strip of lawn about twenty yards wide. The tall figure of a man came jerkily out of the tree shadow as she passed. There was enough starlight and other light for me to make out something extended in one hand and that his face was covered except for the eyes and mouth. Gun and ski mask. Mugger.

I hit the door handle with my left hand, jammed my right up under the dash, and yanked loose the .38 I keep clipped there. He was ten yards from her and closing as I came out of the car; she'd heard him and was turning toward him. He lunged forward, clawing for her purse.

There were no cars on the street. I charged across at an angle, yelling at the top of my voice the only words that can have an effect in a situation like this: "Hold it, police!" Not this time. His head swiveled in my direction, swiveled back to the woman as she pulled away from him. She made a keening noise and turned to run.

He shot her.

No compunction: just threw the gun up and fired point-blank.

She went down, skidding on her side, as I cut through two parked cars onto the sidewalk. Rage made me pull up and I would have fired at him except that he pumped a round at me first. I saw the muzzle flash, heard the whine of the bullet and the low, flat crack of the gun, and in reflex I dodged sideways onto the lawn. Mistake, because the grass was slippery and my feet went out from under me. I stayed down, squirming around on my belly so I could bring the .38 into firing position. But he wasn't going to stick around for a shootout; he was already running splayfooted toward the trees. He disappeared into them before I could get lined up for a shot.

I'd banged my knee in the fall; it sent out twinges as I hauled myself erect, ran toward the woman. She was still down but not hurt as badly as I'd feared: sitting up on one hip now, holding her left arm cradled in against her breast. She heard me, looked up with fright shining on the pale oval of her face. I said quickly, "It's all right, I'm a detective, he's gone now," and shoved the .38 into my jacket pocket. There was no sign of the mugger. The park was empty as far as I could see, no movement anywhere in the warm dark.

She said, "He shot me," in a dazed voice.

"Where? Where are you hurt?"

"My arm . . ."

"Shoulder area?"

"No, above the elbow."

"Can you move the arm?"

"I don't . . . yes, I can move it."

Not too bad then. "Can you stand up, walk?"

"If you help me . . ."

I put an arm around her waist, lifted her. The blood was visible then, gleaming wetly on the sleeve of her sweater.

"My purse," she said.

It was lying on the sidewalk nearby. I let go of her long enough to pick it up. When I gave it to her she clutched it tightly: something solid and familiar to hang onto.

The street was still empty; so were the sidewalks on both sides. Somebody was standing behind a lighted window in one of the buildings across Church, peering through a set of drapes. No one else seemed to have heard the shots, or to want to know what had happened if they did.

Just the woman and me out here at the edge of the light. And the predators—one predator, anyway—hiding somewhere in the dark.

Her name was Andrea Hull, she said, and she lived a few doors up 19th Street. I took her home, walking with my arm around her and her body braced against mine as if we were a pair of lovers. Get her off the street as quickly as possible, to where she would feel safe. I could report the shooting from there. You have to go through the motions even when there's not much chance of results.

Her building was a one-story, stucco-faced duplex. As we started up the front stoop, she drew a shuddering breath and said, "God, he could have killed me," as if the realization had just struck her. "I could be dead right now."

I had nothing to say to that.

"Peter was right, damn him," she said.

"Peter?"

"My husband. He keeps telling me not to go out walking alone at night and I keep not listening. I'm so smart, I am. Nothing ever happened, I thought nothing ever would . . ."

"You learned a lesson," I said. "Don't hurt yourself any more than you already are."

"I hate it when he's right." We were in the vestibule now. She said, "It's the door on the left," and fumbled in her purse. "Where the hell did I put the damn keys?"

"Your husband's not home?"

"No. He's the reason I went out."

I found the keys for her, unlocked the door. Narrow hallway, a huge lighted room opening off it. The room had been enlarged by knocking out a wall or two. There was furniture in it but it wasn't a living room; most of it, with the aid of tall windows and a couple of skylights, had been turned into an artist's studio. A cluttered one full of paintings and sculptures and the tools to create them. An unclean one populated by a tribe of dust mice.

I took a better look at its owner as we entered the studio. Older than I'd first thought, at least thirty-five, maybe forty. A sharp-featured brunette with bright, wise eyes and pale lips. The wound in her arm was still bleeding, the red splotch grown to the size of a small pancake.

"Are you in much pain?" I asked her.

"No. It's mostly numb."

"You'd better get out of that sweater. Put some peroxide on the wound if you have it, then wrap a wet towel around it. That should do until the paramedics get here. Where's your phone?"

"Over by the windows."

"You go ahead. I'll call the police."

". . . I thought *you* were a policeman."

"Not quite. Private investigator."

"What were you doing down by the park?"

"Waiting to serve a subpoena."

"Lord," she said. Then she asked, "Do you have to report what happened? They'll never catch the man, you know they won't."

"Maybe not, but yes, I have to report it. You want attention for that arm, don't you?"

"All right," she said. "Actually, I suppose the publicity will do me some good." She went away through a doorway at the rear.

I made the call. The cop I spoke to asked half a dozen pertinent questions, then told me to stay put, paramedics and a team of inspectors would be out shortly. Half-hour, maybe less, for the paramedics, I thought as I hung up. Longer for the inspectors. This wasn't an A-priority shooting. Perp long gone, victim not seriously wounded, situation under control. We'd just have to wait our turn.

I took a turn around the studio. The paintings were everywhere, finished and unfinished: covering the walls, propped in corners and on a pair of easels, stacked on the floor. They were all abstracts: bold lines and interlocking and overlapping squares, wedges, and triangles in primary colors. Not to my taste, but they appeared to have been done by a talented artist. You couldn't say the same for the forty or so bronze, clay, and metal sculptures. All of those struck me as amateurish, lopsided things that had no identity or meaning, like the stuff kids make free-form in grade school.

"Do you like them? My paintings?"

I turned. Andrea Hull had come back into the room, wearing a sleeveless blouse now, a thick towel wrapped around her arm.

"Still bleeding?" I asked her.

"Not so badly now. *Do* you like my paintings?"

"I don't know much about art, but they seem very good."

"They are. Geometric abstraction. Not as good as Mondrian or Glarner or Burgoyne Diller, perhaps. Or Hofmann, of course. But not derivative, either. I have my own unique vision."

She might have been speaking a foreign language. I said, "Uh-huh," and let it go at that.

"I've had several showings, been praised by some of the most eminent critics in the art world. I'm starting to make a serious name for myself—finally, after years of struggle. Just last month one of my best works, 'Tension and Emotion,' sold for fifteen thousand dollars."

"That's a lot of money."

"Yes, but my work will bring much more someday."

No false modesty in her. Hell, no modesty of any kind. "Are the sculptures yours too?"

She made a snorting noise. "Good God, no. My husband's. Peter thinks he's a brilliant sculptor but he's not—he's not even mediocre. Self-delusion is just one of his faults."

"Sounds like you don't get along very well."

"Sometimes we do. And sometimes he makes me so damn mad I could scream. Tonight, for instance. Calling me from some bar downtown, drunk, bragging about a woman he'd picked up. He *knows* that drives me crazy."

"Uh-huh."

"Oh, not the business with the woman. Another one of his lies, probably. It's the drinking and the taunting that gets to me—his jealousy. He's so damned jealous I swear his skin is developing a green tint."

"Of your success, you mean?"

"That's right."

"Why do you stay married to him if he has that effect on you?"

"Habit," she said. "There's not much love left, but I do still care for him. God knows why. And of course he stays because now there's money, with plenty more in the offing . . . *oh!* Damn!" She'd made the mistake of trying to gesture with her wounded arm. "Where're those paramedics?"

"They'll be here pretty quick."

"I need a drink. Or don't you think I should have one?"

"I wouldn't. They'll give you something for the pain."

"Well, they'd better hurry up. How about you? Do you want a drink?"

"No thanks."

"Suit yourself. Go ahead and sit down if you want. I'm too restless."

"I've been doing nothing but sitting most of the evening."

"I'm going to pace," she said. "I have to walk, keep moving, when I'm upset. I used to go into the park, walk for an hour or more, but with all the drug problems . . . and now a person isn't even safe on the sidewalk—"

There was a rattling at the front door. Andrea Hull turned, scowling, in that direction. I heard the door open, bang closed; a male voice called, "Andrea?"

"In here, Peter."

The man who came duck-waddling in from the hall was a couple of inches over six feet, fair-haired, and pale except for red-blotched cheeks and forehead. Weak-chinned and nervous-eyed. He blinked at her, blinked at me, blinked at her again with his mouth falling open.

"My God, Andrea, what happened to you? That towel . . . there's blood on it . . . ."

"I was mugged a few minutes ago. He shot me."

"*Shot* you? Who . . . ?"

"I told you, a mugger. I'm lucky to be alive."

"The wound . . . it's not serious . . . ?"

"No." She winced. "What's *keeping* those paramedics?"

He went to her, tried to wrap an arm around her shoulders. She pushed him away. "The man who did it," he said, "did you get a good look at him?"

"No. He was masked. This man chased him off."

Hull remembered me, turned, and came waddling over to where I was. "Thank God you were nearby," he said. He breathed on me, reaching for my hand. I let him have it but not for long. "But I don't think I've seen you before. Do you live in the neighborhood?"

"He's a private investigator," Andrea Hull said. "He was serving a subpoena on somebody. His name is Orenzi."

"No, it isn't," I said. I told them what it was, not that either of them cared.

"I can never get Italian names right," she said.

Her husband shifted his attention her way again. "Where did it happen? Down by the park, I'll bet. You went out walking by the park again."

"Don't start in, Peter, I'm in no mood for it."

"Didn't I warn you something like this might happen? A hundred times I've warned you but you just won't listen."

"I said don't start in. If you hadn't called drunk from that bar, got me upset, I wouldn't have gone out. It's as much your fault as it is mine."

"*My* fault? Oh sure, blame me. Twist everything around so you don't have to take responsibility."

Her arm was hurting her and the pain made her vicious. She bared her teeth at him. "What are you doing home, anyway? Where's the bimbo you claimed you picked up?"

"I brushed her off. I kept thinking about what I said on the phone, what a jerk I was being. I wanted to apologize—"

"Sure, right. You were drunk, now you're sober; if there was any brushing off, she's the one who did it."

"Andrea . . ."

"What's the matter with your face? She give you some kind of rash?"

"My face? There's nothing wrong with my face . . ."

"It looks like a rash. I hope it isn't contagious."

"Damn you, Andrea—"

I'd had enough of this. The bickering, the hatred, the deception—everything about the two of them and their not-so-private little war. I said sharply; "All right, both of you shut up. I'm tired of listening to you."

They gawked at me, the woman in disbelief. "How dare you. You can't talk to me like that in my own home—"

"I can and I will. Keep your mouth closed and your ears open for five minutes and you'll learn something. Your husband and I will do the talking."

Hull said, "I don't have anything to say to you."

"Sure you do, Peter. You can start by telling me what you did with the gun."

"Gun? I don't. . . what gun?"

"The one you shot your wife with."

Him: hissing intake of breath.

Her: strangled bleating noise.

"That's right. No mugger, just you trying to take advantage of what's happened to the park and the neighborhood, make it look like a street killing."

Him: "That's a lie, a damn lie!"

Her, to me, in a ground-glass voice: "Peter? How can you know it was Peter? It was dark, the man wore a mask . . ."

"For openers, you told me he was drunk when he called you earlier. He wasn't, he was faking it. Nobody can sober up completely in an hour, not when he's standing here now without the faintest smell of alcohol on his breath. He wasn't downtown, either; he was somewhere close-by. The call was designed to upset you so you'd do what you usually do when you're upset—go out for a walk by the park.

"It may have been dark, but I still got a pretty good look at the shooter coming and going. Tall—and Peter's tall. Walked and ran splayfooted, like a duck—and that's how Peter walks. Then there are those blotches on his face. It's not a rash; look at the marks closely, Mrs. Hull. He's got the kind of skin that takes and retains imprints from fabric, right? Wakes up in the morning with pillow and blanket marks on his face? The ones he's got now are exactly the kind the ribbing on a ski mask would leave."

"You son of a bitch," she said to him. "You dirty rotten son of a—"

She went for him with nails flashing. I got in her way, grabbed hold of her; her injured arm stopped her from struggling with me. Then he tried to make a run for it. I let go of her and chased him and caught him at the front door. When he tried to kick me I knocked him on his skinny tail.

And with perfect timing, the doorbell rang. It wasn't just the paramedics, either; the law had also arrived.

Peter Hull was an idiot. He had the gun, a .32 revolver, *and* the ski mask in the trunk of his car.

She pressed charges, of course. She would have cut his throat with a dull knife if they'd let her have one. She told him so, complete with expletives.

The Hulls and their private war were finished.

Down in Dolores Park—and in the other neighborhoods in the city, and in cities throughout the country—the other war, the big one, goes on. Armageddon? Maybe. And maybe the forces of evil *are* winning. Not in the long run, though. In the long run, the forces of good will triumph. Always have, always will.

If I didn't believe that, I couldn't work at my job. Neither could anybody else in law enforcement.

No matter how bad things seem, we can't ever stop believing it.

LIAR'S DICE

EXCUSE ME. Do you play liar's dice?"

I looked over at the man two stools to my right. He was about my age, early forties: average height, average weight, brown hair, medium complexion—really a pretty nondescript sort except for a pleasant and disarming smile. Expensively dressed in an Armani suit and a silk jacquard tie. Drinking white wine. I had never seen him before. Or had I? There was something familiar about him, as if our paths *had* crossed somewhere or other, once or twice.

Not here in Tony's, though. Tony's is a suburban-mall bar that caters to the shopping trade from the big department and grocery stores surrounding it. I stopped in no more than a couple of times a month, usually when Connie asked me to pick up something at Safeway on my way home from San Francisco, occasionally when I had a Saturday errand to run. I knew the few regulars by sight, and it was never very crowded anyway. There were only four patrons at the moment: the nondescript gent and myself on stools, and a young couple in a booth at the rear.

"I do play, as a matter of fact," I said to the fellow. Fairly well too, though I wasn't about to admit that. Liar's dice and I were old acquaintances.

"Would you care to shake for a drink?"

"Well, my usual limit is one . . ."

"For a chit for your next visit, then."

"All right, why not? I feel lucky tonight."

"Do you? Good. I should warn you, I'm very good at the game."

"I'm not so bad myself."

"No, I mean I'm *very* good. I seldom lose."

It was the kind of remark that would have nettled me if it had been said with even a modicum of conceit. But he wasn't bragging; he was merely stating a fact, mentioning a special skill of which he felt justifiably proud. So instead of annoying me, his comment made me eager to test him.

We introduced ourselves; his name was Jones. Then I called to Tony for the dice cups. He brought them down, winked at me, said, "No gambling now," and went back to the other end of the bar. Strictly speaking, shaking dice for drinks and/or money is illegal in California. But nobody pays much attention to nuisance laws like that, and most bar owners keep dice cups on hand for their customers. The game stimulates business. I know because I've been involved in some spirited liar's dice tournaments in my time.

Like all good games, liar's dice is fairly simple—at least in its rules. Each player has a cup containing five dice, which he shakes out but keeps covered so only he can see what is showing face up. Then each makes a declaration or "call" in turn: one of a kind, two of a kind, three of a kind, and so on. Each call has to be higher than the previous one, and is based on what the player *knows* is in his hand and what he *thinks* is in the other fellow's—the combined total of the ten dice. He can lie or tell the truth, whichever suits him; but the better liar he is, the better his chances of winning. When one player decides the other is either lying or has simply exceeded the laws of probability, he says, "Come up," and then both reveal their hands. If he's right, he wins.

In addition to being a clever liar, you also need a good grasp of mathematical odds and the ability to "read" your opponent's facial expressions, the inflection in his voice, his body language. The same skills an experienced poker player has to have, which is one reason the game is also called liar's poker.

Jones and I each rolled one die to determine who would go first; mine was the highest. Then we shook all five dice in our cups, banged them down on the bar. What I had showing was four treys and a deuce.

"Your call, Mr. Quint."

"One five," I said.

"One six."

"Two deuces."

"Two fives."

"Three treys."

"Three sixes."

I considered calling him up, since I had no sixes and he would need three showing to win. But I didn't know his methods and I couldn't read him at all. I decided to keep playing.

"Four treys."

"Five treys."

"Six treys."

Jones smiled and said, "Come up." And he had just one trey (and no sixes). I'd called six treys and there were only five in our combined hands; he was the winner.

"So much for feeling lucky," I said, and signaled Tony to bring another white wine for Mr. Jones. On impulse I decided a second Manhattan wouldn't hurt me and ordered that too.

Jones said, "Shall we play again?"

"Two drinks is definitely my limit."

"For dimes, then? Nickels or pennies, if you prefer."

"Oh, I don't know . . ."

"You're a good player, Mr. Quint, and I don't often find someone who can challenge me. Besides, I have a passion as well as an affinity for liar's dice. Won't you indulge me?"

I didn't see any harm in it. If he'd wanted to play for larger stakes, even a dollar a hand, I might have taken him for a hustler despite his Armani suit and silk tie. But how much could you win or lose playing for a nickel or a dime a hand? So I said, "Your call first this time," and picked up my dice cup.

We played for better than half an hour. And Jones wasn't just good; he was uncanny. Out of nearly twenty-five hands, I won two—*two.* You could chalk up some of the disparity to luck, but not enough to change the fact that his skill was remarkable. Certainly he was the best I'd ever locked horns with. I would have backed him in a tournament anywhere, anytime.

He was a good winner, too: no gloating or chiding. And a good listener, the sort who seems genuinely (if superficially) interested in other people. I'm not often gregarious, especially with strangers, but I found myself opening up to Jones—and this in spite of him beating the pants off me the whole time.

I told him about Connie, how we met and the second honeymoon trip we'd taken to Lake Louise three years ago and what we were planning for our twentieth wedding anniversary in August. I told him about Lisa, who was eighteen and a freshman studying film at UCLA. I told him about Kevin, sixteen now and captain of his high school baseball team, and the five-hit, two-home run game he'd had last week. I told him what it was like working as a design engineer for one of the largest engineering firms in the country, the nagging dissatisfaction and the desire to be my own boss someday, when I had enough money saved so I could afford to take the risk. I told him about remodeling our home, the boat I was thinking of buying, the fact that I'd always wanted to try hang gliding but never had the courage.

Lord knows what else I might have told him if I hadn't noticed the polite but faintly bored expression on his face, as if I were imparting facts he already knew. It made me realize just how much I'd been nattering on, and embarrassed me a bit. I've never liked people who talk incessantly about themselves, as though they're the focal point of the entire universe. I can be a good listener myself; and for all I knew, Jones was a lot more interesting than bland Jeff Quint.

I said, "Well, that's more than enough about me. It's your turn, Jones. Tell me about yourself."

"If you like, Mr. Quint." Still very formal. I'd told him a couple of times to call me Jeff but he wouldn't do it. Now that I thought about it, he hadn't mentioned his own first name.

"What is it you do?"

He laid his dice cup to one side. I was relieved to see that; I'd had enough of losing but I hadn't wanted to be the one to quit. And it was getting late—dark outside already—and Connie would be wondering where I was. A few minutes of listening to the story of his life, I thought, just to be polite, and then—

"To begin with," Jones was saying, "I travel."

"Sales job?"

"No. I travel because I enjoy traveling. And because I can afford it. I have independent means."

"Lucky you. In more ways than one."

"Yes."

"Europe, the South Pacific—all the exotic places?"

"Actually, no. I prefer the U.S."

"Any particular part?"

"Wherever my fancy leads me."

"Hard to imagine anyone's fancy leading him to Bayport," I said. "You have friends or relatives here?"

"No, I have business in Bayport."

"Business? I thought you said you didn't need to work . . ."

"Independent means, Mr. Quint. That doesn't preclude a purpose, a direction in one's life."

"You do have a profession, then?"

"You might say that. A profession and a hobby combined."

"Lucky you," I said again. "What is it?"

"I kill people," he said.

I thought I'd misheard him. "You . . . what?"

"I kill people."

"Good God. Is that supposed to be a joke?"

"Not at all. I'm quite serious."

"What do you mean, you *kill* people?"

"Just what I said."

"Are you trying to tell me you're . . . some kind of paid assassin?"

"Not at all. I've never killed anyone for money."

"Then why . . .?"

"Can't you guess?"

"No, I can't guess. I don't want to guess."

"Call it personal satisfaction," he said.

"What people? Who?"

"No one in particular," Jones said. "My selection process is completely random. I'm very good at it too. I've been killing people for. . . let's see, nine and a half years now. Eighteen victims in thirteen states. And, oh yes, Puerto Rico—one in Puerto Rico. I don't mind saying that I've never even come close to being caught."

I stared at him. My mouth was open; I knew it but I couldn't seem to unlock my jaw. I felt as if reality had suddenly slipped away from me, as if Tony had dropped some sort of mind-altering drug into my second Manhattan and it was just now taking effect. Jones and I were still sitting companionably, on adjacent stools now, he smiling and speaking in the same low, friendly voice. At the other end of the bar Tony was slicing lemons and limes into wedges. Three of the booths were occupied now, with people laughing and enjoying themselves. Everything was just as it had been two minutes ago, except that instead of me telling Jones about being a dissatisfied design engineer, he was calmly telling me he was a serial murderer.

I got my mouth shut finally, just long enough to swallow into a dry throat. Then I said, "You're crazy, Jones. You must be insane."

"Hardly, Mr. Quint. I'm as sane as you are."

"I don't believe you killed eighteen people."

"Nineteen," he said. "Soon to be twenty."

"Twenty? You mean . . . someone in Bayport?"

"Right here in Bayport."

"You expect me to believe you intend to pick somebody at random and just . . . murder him in cold blood?"

"Oh no, there's more to it than that. Much more."

"More?" I said blankly.

"I choose a person at random, yes, but carefully. Very carefully. I study my target, follow him as he goes about his daily business, learn everything I can about him, down to the minutest detail. Then the cat and mouse begins. I don't murder him right away; that wouldn't give sufficient, ah, satisfaction. I wait . . . observe . . . plan. Perhaps, for added spice, I reveal myself to him. I might even be so bold as to tell him to his face that he's my next victim."

My scalp began to crawl.

"Days, weeks . . . then, when the victim least expects it, a gunshot, a push out of nowhere in front of an oncoming car, a hypodermic filled with digitalin and jabbed into the body on a crowded street, simulating heart failure. There are many ways to kill a man. Did you ever stop to consider just how many different ways there are?"

"You . . . you're not saying—"

"What, Mr. Quint? That I've chosen *you?* "

"Jones, for God's sake!"

"But I have," he said. "You are to be number twenty."

One of my hands jerked upward, struck his arm. Involuntary spasm; I'm not a violent man. He didn't even flinch. I pulled my hand back, saw that it was shaking, and clutched the fingers tight around the beveled edge of the bar.

Jones took a sip of wine. Then he smiled—and winked at me.

"Or then again," he said, "I might be lying."

". . . What?"

"Everything I've just told you might be a lie. I might not have killed nineteen people over the past nine and a half years; I might not have killed anyone, ever."

"I don't. . . I don't know what you—"

"Or I might have told you part of the truth . . . that's another possibility, isn't it? Part fact, part fiction. But in that case, which is which? And to what degree? Am I a deadly threat to you, or am I nothing more than a man in a bar playing a game?"

"Game? What kind of sick—"

"The same one we've been playing all along. Liar's dice."

"Liar's . . . ?"

"My own special version," he said, "developed and refined through years of practice. The perfect form of the game, if I do say so myself—exciting, unpredictable, filled with intrigue and mortal danger for myself as well as my opponent."

I shook my head. My mind was a seething muddle; I couldn't seem to fully grasp what he was saying.

"I don't know any more than you do at this moment how you'll play your part of the hand, Mr. Quint. That's where the excitement and the danger lies. Will you treat what I've said as you would a bluff? Can you afford to take that risk? Or will you act on the assumption that I've told the truth, or at least part of it?"

"Damn you . . ." Weak and ineffectual words, even in my own ears.

"And if you do believe me," he said, "what course of action will you take? Attack me before I can harm you, attempt to kill me . . . here and now in this public place, perhaps, in front of witnesses who will swear the attack was unprovoked? Try to follow me when I leave, attack me elsewhere? I might be armed, and an excellent shot with a handgun. Go to the police . . . with a wild-sounding and unsubstantiated story that they surely wouldn't believe? Hire a detective to track me down? Attempt to track me down yourself? Jones isn't my real name, of course, and I've taken precautions against anyone finding out my true identity. Arm yourself and remain on guard until, if and when, I make a move against you? How long could you live under such intense pressure without making a fatal mistake?"

He paused dramatically. "Or—and this is the most exciting prospect of all, the one I hope you choose—will you mount a clever counterattack, lies and deceptions of your own devising? Can you actually hope to beat me at my own game? Do you dare to try?"

He adjusted the knot in his tie with quick, deft movements, smiling at me in the back-bar mirror—not the same pleasant smile as before. This one had shark's teeth in it. "Whatever you do, I'll know about it soon afterward. I'll be waiting . . . watching . . . and I'll know. And then it will be my turn again."

He slid off his stool, stood poised behind me. I just sat there; it was as if I were paralyzed.

"Your call, Mr. Quint," he said. And he was gone into the night.

OLAF AND THE MERCHANDISERS

(with Barry N. Malzberg)

O LAF IMAGINES better times while he watches sports action rumble, commercials and promos tumble. This time-out brought to you by Father Time Timepiece, "you'll never be late for the march with Father Time," this call to bullpen sponsored by Hokura Cellular, "the whole wide world of technology in the palm of your hand," this picture of bleeding toothless hockey defenseman in penalty box brought to you by rumble tumble bumble sponsors who bring you everything else on Sports Channels I through XII.

Old Olaf steams with rage as sports, commercials, promos continue unabated in his two-bedroom furnished, heat and hot water extra, no charge for cockroaches. Olaf's legs hurt, hips hurt, back twinges every two minutes regular as if atrophied muscles attached to timer. He can't sit long without standing, can't stand long without sitting. TV sports are all Olaf has left in his misguided life. Twelve sports channels on cheap cable; he switches back and forth, forth and back, back and forth.

Ravens versus Colts, 34-7 Colts in the third quarter, game brought to you by Steinmetz Gold, world's finest hops and barley, chill-brewed in special vats, "it's liquid gold in your glass." Greater Cleveland golf tournament, Miller and Deloach tied for lead at six-under, Deloach in rough on back nine, Miller with 40-foot putt for birdie to take the lead, but first a word from our sponsor, Derry's Restaurants, Hungry Folks' Breakfast $2.99 every day all day. World skateboard finals live from Fiji, courtesy of Polynesian Airlines, "a taste of paradise in the sky." Championship tennis, Turgenov versus King, Turgenov leads two sets to one, 40-love in fourth set, serves ace for game set match, match brought to you by Matchmaker Inc., "matchmaker, matchmaker, match my ideal mate." Scores, names, games, commercial messages buzz and flit through recently retired Olaf's brain.

Olaf once believed retirement meant quiet life in two-bedroom furnished, watching live broadcasts of great sports events, analyzing games along with analysts, finding some peace after forty years of dry goods and happenstance and parsing goods of useless existence. But what does he get?

This is what Olaf gets: distraction. Barrage of commercials, assault of spot promos for other sports and for sitcoms, reality shows, game shows, news shows. Olaf feels like old ugly animal in zoo cage, bombarded and insulted by talking heads, products and services and laugh tracks and prime-time time wasters hurled at him like stones. TV's highest rated show, funniest sitcom ever, coaches' roundtable, Joe Bob's Best Sports Moments, WWF Bonecrush Facedown; loudest, sexiest, silliest, most thrilling, most informative. Monster truck demolition derby brought to you by New Millennium Insurance, "our claims back up your claims." Olaf sits, Olaf stands, Olaf suffers in angry solitude. Game recap brought to you by Happyland Pleasure World, "fun in the Florida sun for the entire family." Olaf's life recap brought to you by Storr's Premium Lite and Analgesic Double Plus Pain Reliever.

Here is the life of Olaf Thorkelssen: Born in St. Paul, Minnesota same year John F. Kennedy elected president. Good student with many insights, many plans for future as business entrepreneur. Migrated east at age eighteen to attend college, met Mary Jo Petersen from Yonkers in sophomore year, got her pregnant first time in after drunken frat party. Olaf did right thing, quit school, married Mary Jo, took job with Plume Dry Goods Inc. Fathered second child bang-bang, bought house, worked hard, lived conventional life. Children grew up, moved out, devout daughter Clarice married Baptist minister in Indianapolis, drug-freak son Vernon (named after wife's brother) MIA in California. Olaf sold house for below market value because of poor upkeep, moved with Mary Jo into two-bedroom furnished, retired from Plume Dry Goods. Wanted only solace and peace for declining years, but has been denied same.

One day in two-bedroom furnished Olaf made another mistake in mistake-riddled life. Said to wife why don't kids combine interests, make commercial for religious TV network, get rich. "Today's sermon brought to you by Meth-Ease, the gentle high for pious sinners." Humor-challenged wife burst into tears, said to him "You monster!" and rushed out of room. Olaf thereafter refused dutiful marital relations, despite repeated threats and occasional begging.

After six months inevitable happens. Wife says all Olaf does since retirement is watch TV sports and drink beer, spend all day and half the night in tomb of empty beer cans, announcers' voices and crowd noise and commercials blaring, and she can't take it any more. She moves out, moves in with sister in Hackensack, leaves poor Olaf all alone. Frustrated bitter Olaf thinks he is better off without her.

Olaf now has no one except fat Lou Dinucci. Lou occupies one-bedroom furnished in same building and is also victim of wifely defection, also recently retired from sales job with Fleet Organic Snack Food Company, "Fleet—the elite treat." Sports and Storr's Premium Lite only things Olaf has in common with Lou the mooch, Lou the know-it-all. Every Saturday and Sunday Lou comes over to eat Olaf's food, quaff Olaf's beer, make Olaf's miserable life more miserable.

Here is what Olaf and Lou do together: watch sports, drink flavorful, noncaloric brew, argue about Celebrity Bowling brought to you by New Age Burgers, "the fast food of the future," and NFL Game of the Century brought to you by Hansen's Fine Stuffed BBQ Chicken Breasts, "we fill 'em, you grill 'em," and Championship Pool sponsored by Big Fellows, "the natural sexual enhancement for the man on the rise." Argue about college football and pro football and soccer and baseball and basketball and hockey and track and field and gymnastics and croquet and curling and sumo wrestling. Argue about types of deodorant, headache remedies, radial tires, American cars, Japanese cars, German cars, hair replacement methods, potato chips, microwave popcorn, cheese (Wisconsin has the best, no California, no England, no Holland), and brands of ketchup, mustard, pickles, soup, soap, and packaged nuts. Fat Lou, arrogant Lou, says if he makes it to heaven he'll argue with God about nature of the universe. Conflicted Olaf hates long hours spent with loudmouth nonfriend, looks forward to them at the same time.

One Sunday Olaf is seized by sudden idea in the middle of whick-whack hi-team women's beach volleyball semifinals from beautiful island of Maui, brought to you by Sun-Oil Sixteen, "as gentle as a lover's touch on sensitive skin." Excited, he stands up to ease pain in aching back and hips, says to Lou, "Brilliant money-making concept just came to me. How about we start a brand-new TV sports event?"

Lou struggles to position of attention. "There is no new sports event," he says. "All sports are already on TV."

"Darts," Olaf says.

"Darts? Did you say darts?"

"Organized series of championship dart tournaments. Beginning at local level, moving on through increasing attention and
popularity to national prominence on cable sports channel, title
match brought to you by Old England Dart Boards or other related
corporate sponsor."

"Look at the ass on that blonde," Lou says, staring at the TV
screen.

"World Series of Darts," Olaf says. "No, better yet, International Darts Federation Tournament of Champions."

"Best asses in TV sports in beach volleyball matches," Lou
says.

"It's a brilliant concept and you know it," Olaf says.

"Not brilliant, stupid." Lou listens to the announcer say Rocky
Mountain Ice Beer, "no brew colder south of Alaska," is best of all
American beers. "Garbage," he says. "Storr's Premium Lite is the
best, the coldest, any fool knows that."

"Darts," Olaf says.

"I don't know anything about darts," Lou says. "You don't
know anything about darts. Who cares about darts?"

"Patrons in bars. Darts is a very big game in bars."

"To play, not to watch on TV. Darts is not a big-audience
game."

"Beach volleyball isn't a big audience game either," Olaf points
out. "Nobody in Minnesota plays beach volleyball, yet viewers in
Minneapolis and St. Paul are watching beach volleyball this very
moment same as we are. It's all promotion."

"No ocean beaches in Minnesota," Lou says wisely.

"We'll make millions with the right promotion, right sponsors,
right TV channel," Olaf says. "Sports Channel X, home of Xtreme
toboggan racing, is perfect for International Darts Federation
Tournament of Champions."

"Another slice of crazy Olaf pie," Lou says and shakes his head
in disdain. "Volleyball asses far more interesting than darts any
day."

Olaf tries not to look at volleyball asses. He is not too old for
sex; thoughts of blonde beach girls are very disturbing. "Brilliant
concept," he says. "Golden goose eggs."

"Goose eggs, all right, but not golden." Lou stirs, belches,
heaves to his feet as commercial break for Sun-Oil Sixteen inter-
rupts volleyball match in the middle of hard whick-whack spike by
another blonde beach girl. "Suppose we go down to O'Ryan's, ask
him what he thinks?"

Cunning Olaf doesn't argue with this. Olaf knows O'Ryan, once drank many Storr's Premium Lites in The Rose of Shannon Irish Pub before his back and hips hurt too much for long hours of perching on bar stool. O'Ryan is a very wise man, knows more about sports than anybody in Yonkers, has connections with local TV station. O'Ryan will be Olaf's ally and perhaps not so silent partner in great darts venture.

Soon stooped aching Olaf and fat smart-mouth Lou are in The Rose of Shannon Irish Pub, Olaf making direct appeal to O'Ryan whose actual name is Isidore Gomfrey. Upon transfer of bar ownership from the O'Ryan family, he adopted O'Ryan name as what they call in the trade his working moniker. O'Ryan listens to Olaf's brilliant proposal for International Darts Federation Tournament of Champions. Nods, considers. Olaf leans forward, expectant, dollar signs and vague beach girl images dancing merrily through his head. "Well?" he says. "What do you think?"

"I think you're crazy," O'Ryan says.

"What?"

"Darts is not a big audience game."

Lou makes noise like a chortling rabbit.

"No money in darts," O'Ryan says. "Nobody cares about darts except drunks throwing for beers in dark corners of The Rose of Shannon."

Olaf and Lou return to two-bedroom furnished, Olaf percolating with rage and humiliation. Lou makes a fool of him, Isadore Gomfrey makes a fool of him, life makes a fool of him. Olaf the maligned, Olaf the doomed failure. Nothing he thinks or plans or does ever turns out right, even brilliant darts concept; he must be cursed by capricious gods who single him out for special torture.

Angry Olaf and chortling Lou sit-stand and sip suds, watching six-man helmetless Xtreme Toboggan Racing teams engage in thrilling, dangerous competition brought to you by Hilfinger's Custom Sleighs, "we'll give you the ride of your life." Is toboggan racing a big-audience sport? Olaf wonders. One toboggan crashes into wall, caroms off, spills helmetless men onto ice slide. Announcers very excited, Lou very excited, until snowmist clears to show none of the spilled tobogganers badly hurt in the crash. "Damn," Lou says. Plenty of mayhem and broken bones in Xtreme Toboggan Racing, Olaf thinks; that must be the reason for big-audience appeal on Sports Channel X. No mayhem and broken bones in darts tournament, unless maybe opposing contestants have boards strapped on their heads to catch thrown darts like William Tell with apple and arrows.

Olaf says this to Lou, who laughs so hard his jowls wobble like gobs of vanilla pudding. "Crazy Olaf," he says. "Forget about darts and crack me another brew. Time for the big game to start."

Olaf yearns to tell Lou to crack his own brew, bring his own brew next time, but he doesn't. Weak spineless Olaf does Lou's bidding.

Big game today is Giants versus Jets from RingTech Computer Software Company Stadium, formerly Giants Stadium, brought to you by ShellEx Petroleum, "our gas is your gas," and Steinmetz Gold, and hot powerful new American Zephyr Z-8 sports coupe, "all new safety features and fastest zero to sixty acceleration of any passenger car ever built." Most important game of NFL season, winner likely to play undefeated former expansion Daytona Bulldogs in Super Bowl XLXIV in Mexico City.

"Giants by two touchdowns," Lou says confidently.

"Jets," Olaf says. "Jets by seven."

"Bobby Immelman is best quarterback in the NFL."

"John Jay Finkelhammer has better stats."

"Immelman has better touchdown to interception passing ratio and more last-minute come-from-behind victories than John Elway. Best pro quarterback ever to play for a New York team."

"No, Joe Namath, bad knees and all, was the best ever. Namath should be in the Hall of Fame."

Lou emits a derisive laugh, quaffs beer, licks foam off his upper lip like a cat licks cream, throws empty can onto pile on floor. "Namath was one-year phenom," he says, "Super Bowl hero but regular season bum."

Olaf feels rage come back. Argue, argue, argue, and he never wins even one time. Olaf deserves better than this, a better friend than loudmouth retired snack-hack salesman, a happier post-retirement existence. But Olaf's life is a tattered tapestry woven of hangovers and back pain and Saturday and Sunday arguments and five minutes of commercials to every one minute of top sports action. Olaf is fresh out of options, fresh out of future prospects.

Game starts, game progresses. Rumble tumble fumble. American Zephyr and Steinmetz Gold and Foot-Long Hot Links, "livin' high on the hog with the big dog." Giants lead 17-10 at halftime, lead 24-13 middle of third quarter. Jets go on offense, drive to Giants' 47 yard line. John Jay Finkelhammer rolls out, can't find open receiver, is swarmed over by six huge Giants' defensive linemen. Players unpile, John Jay Finkelhammer doesn't get up.

"Hurt," Lou says. "Look at instant replay. Hurt bad."

"No," Olaf says.

"Yes," Lou says. "This could be worst sports injury on TV ever."

"Worst sports injury on TV ever Joe Thiesmann's broken leg, Giants versus Redskins, RFK Stadium, November 1985."

"Wrong," Lou says. "Until today, worst sports injury on TV ever Jerome 'Slammer' Marshall's broken neck, Knicks versus Celtics, Madison Square Garden, June 2012. Slammer dove for a loose ball, jammed his head into scorer's table, spent three hundred and six days in a coma before they yanked his feeding tube."

Angry Olaf swallows more beer. Foamy brew passes straight through to his bladder so fast he almost doesn't reach the bathroom in time for usual trickle, wiggle, spurt and squirt. Olaf makes painful way back to living room, hears TV announcer say John Jay Finkelhammer still not moving, situation looks bad, could be very serious injury.

"Didn't I tell you?" Lou says, staring raptly at the screen. "Worst sports injury on TV ever."

"Finkelhammer is a very tough competitor," Olaf says. "He'll get up pretty soon, lead Jets to fourth-quarter victory."

"Wrong on both counts, as usual." Lou belches, farts. His face seems to grow bigger, wider, to open up like a white poisonous flower with a wet red center. "Finkelhammer may never get up again."

Olaf's rage grows and grows, assumes Viking proportions. Something goes click-clack, whick-whack in his head. Darts farts Zephyr Steinmetz bowling golf Bonecrush Facedown volleyball asses Fleet Fleet elite treat fill 'em grill 'em matchmaker matchmaker Hungry Folks' Breakfast high on hog with big dog Namath Slammer Finkelhammer best beer worst injury crazy Olaf hateful Lou rumble tumble mumble. Olaf gets up, goes into bedroom, finds cunningly hidden weapon bought long ago to repel intruders, goes back to living room.

Fat noxious Lou is still staring at tube, Storr's Premium Lite can raised in midair. "This might be the end of Finklehammer," he says, excited. "No kidding, I think he's dead."

"I think so too," Olaf says and the gun goes bang bang bang. Bullets punch neat round holes in Storr's can, neat round holes in

Lou Dinucci. Former snack-hack salesman falls over dead in tomb of empty beer cans.

TV announcer says, "This injury timeout brought to you by Mexican Village, home of Gigantico Burrito, 'big enough for two and better than mamacita makes.' "

Olaf Thorkelssen, brilliant creator of International Darts Federation Tournament of Champions, says, "This murder brought to you by Jones and Smith thirty-eight caliber Undercover Model 2015 revolver, 'aims straight, shoots great.' "

Then happy sad crazy like a fox Olaf pops open another brew, changes channels, and watches commercials and promos occasionally interrupted by rumble tumble sports action until police come and take him away.

ABOUT BILL PRONZINI...

A full-time professional writer since 1969, **Bill Pronzini** has published close to 70 novels, including three in collaboration with his wife, novelist **Marcia Muller**, and 33 in his popular "Nameless Detective" series. He is also the author of four nonfiction books, 20 collections of short stories, and scores of uncollected stories, articles, essays, and book reviews; and he has edited or coedited numerous anthologies. His work has been translated into eighteen languages and published in nearly thirty countries.

In 2008 he was named Grand Master by the Mystery Writers of America, the organization's highest award. He has also received three Shamus Awards, two for Best Novel, and the Lifetime Achievement Award (presented in 1987) from the Private Eye Writers of America; and six nominations for MWA's Edgar Allan Poe award. His suspense novel, **Snowbound**, was the recipient of the Grand Prix de la Litterature Policiere as the best crime novel published in France in 1988. Two other suspense novels, **A Wasteland of Strangers** and **The Crimes of Jordan Wise** were nominated for the Hammett Prize for best crime novel of 1997 and 2006 respectively by the International Crime Writers Association. And his young-adult short story, "Christmas Gifts," was the recipient of the Paul A. Witty Award presented by the International Reading Association for the best YA short fiction of 1999.

RAMBLE HOUSE's

HARRY STEPHEN KEELER WEBWORK MYSTERIES

(RH) indicates the title is available ONLY in the RAMBLE HOUSE edition

The Ace of Spades Murder
The Affair of the Bottled Deuce (RH)
The Amazing Web
The Barking Clock
Behind That Mask
The Book with the Orange Leaves
The Bottle with the Green Wax Seal
The Box from Japan
The Case of the Canny Killer
The Case of the Crazy Corpse (RH)
The Case of the Flying Hands (RH)
The Case of the Ivory Arrow
The Case of the Jeweled Ragpicker
The Case of the Lavender Gripsack
The Case of the Mysterious Moll
The Case of the 16 Beans
The Case of the Transparent Nude (RH)
The Case of the Transposed Legs
The Case of the Two-Headed Idiot (RH)
The Case of the Two Strange Ladies
The Circus Stealers (RH)
Cleopatra's Tears
A Copy of Beowulf (RH)
The Crimson Cube (RH)
The Face of the Man From Saturn
Find the Clock
The Five Silver Buddhas
The 4th King
The Gallows Waits, My Lord! (RH)
The Green Jade Hand
Finger! Finger!
Hangman's Nights (RH)
I, Chameleon (RH)
I Killed Lincoln at 10:13! (RH)
The Iron Ring
The Man Who Changed His Skin (RH)
The Man with the Crimson Box
The Man with the Magic Eardrums
The Man with the Wooden Spectacles
The Marceau Case
The Matilda Hunter Murder
The Monocled Monster

The Murder of London Lew
The Murdered Mathematician
The Mysterious Card (RH)
The Mysterious Ivory Ball of Wong Shing Li (RH)
The Mystery of the Fiddling Cracksman
The Peacock Fan
The Photo of Lady X (RH)
The Portrait of Jirjohn Cobb
Report on Vanessa Hewstone (RH)
Riddle of the Travelling Skull
Riddle of the Wooden Parrakeet (RH)
The Scarlet Mummy (RH)
The Search for X-Y-Z
The Sharkskin Book
Sing Sing Nights
The Six From Nowhere (RH)
The Skull of the Waltzing Clown
The Spectacles of Mr. Cagliostro
Stand By—London Calling!
The Steeltown Strangler
The Stolen Gravestone (RH)
Strange Journey (RH)
The Strange Will
The Straw Hat Murders (RH)
The Street of 1000 Eyes (RH)
Thieves' Nights
Three Novellos (RH)
The Tiger Snake
The Trap (RH)
Vagabond Nights (Defrauded Yeggman)
Vagabond Nights 2 (10 Hours)
The Vanishing Gold Truck
The Voice of the Seven Sparrows
The Washington Square Enigma
When Thief Meets Thief
The White Circle (RH)
The Wonderful Scheme of Mr. Christopher Thorne
X. Jones—of Scotland Yard
Y. Cheung, Business Detective

Keeler Related Works

A To Izzard: A Harry Stephen Keeler Companion by Fender Tucker — Articles and stories about Harry, by Harry, and in his style. Included is a compleat bibliography.

Wild About Harry: Reviews of Keeler Novels — Edited by Richard Polt & Fender Tucker — 22 reviews of works by Harry Stephen Keeler from *Keeler News*. A perfect introduction to the author.

The Keeler Keyhole Collection: Annotated newsletter rants from Harry Stephen Keeler, edited by Francis M. Nevins. Over 400 pages of incredibly personal Keeleriana.

Fakealoo — Pastiches of the style of Harry Stephen Keeler by selected demented members of the HSK Society. Updated every year with the new winner.

RAMBLE HOUSE's OTHER LOONS

The End of It All and Other Stories — Ed Gorman's latest short story collection

Four Dancing Tuatara Press Books — *Beast or Man?* By Sean M'Guire; *The Whistling Ancestors* by Richard E. Goddard; *The Shadow on the House* and *Sorcerer's Chessmen* by Mark Hansom. With introductions by John Pelan

The Dumpling — Political murder from 1907 by Coulson Kernahan

Victims & Villains — Intriguing Sherlockiana from Derham Groves

Evidence in Blue — 1938 mystery by E. Charles Vivian

The Case of the Little Green Men — Mack Reynolds wrote this love song to sci-fi fans back in 1951 and it's now back in print.

Hell Fire — A new hard-boiled novel by Jack Moskovitz about an arsonist, an arson cop and a Nazi hooker. It isn't pretty.

Researching American-Made Toy Soldiers — A 276-page collection of a lifetime of articles by toy soldier expert Richard O'Brien

Strands of the Web: Short Stories of Harry Stephen Keeler — Edited and Introduced by Fred Cleaver

The Sam McCain Novels — Ed Gorman's terrific series includes *The Day the Music Died*, *Wake Up Little Susie* and *Will You Still Love Me Tomorrow?*

A Shot Rang Out — Three decades of reviews from Jon Breen

Mysterious Martin, the Master of Murder — Two versions of a strange 1912 novel by Tod Robbins about a man who writes books that can kill.

Dago Red — 22 tales of dark suspense by Bill Pronzini

The Night Remembers — A 1991 Jack Walsh mystery from Ed Gorman

Rough Cut & New, Improved Murder — Ed Gorman's first two novels

Hollywood Dreams — A novel of the Depression by Richard O'Brien

Seven Gelett Burgess Novels — *The Master of Mysteries*, *The White Cat*, *Two O'Clock Courage*, *Ladies in Boxes*, *Find the Woman*, *The Heart Line*, *The Picaroons*

The Organ Reader — A huge compilation of just about everything published in the 1971-1972 radical bay-area newspaper, THE ORGAN.

A Clear Path to Cross — Sharon Knowles short mystery stories by Ed Lynskey

Old Times' Sake — Short stories by James Reasoner from Mike Shayne Magazine

Freaks and Fantasies — Eerie tales by Tod Robbins, collaborator of Tod Browning on the film FREAKS.

Seven Jim Harmon Double Novels — *Vixen Hollow/Celluloid Scandal*, *The Man Who Made Maniacs/Silent Siren*, *Ape Rape/Wanton Witch*, *Sex Burns Like Fire/Twist Session*, *Sudden Lust/Passion Strip*, *Sin Unlimited/Harlot Master*, *Twilight Girls/Sex Institution*. Written in the early 60s.

Marblehead: A Novel of H.P. Lovecraft — A long-lost masterpiece from Richard A. Lupoff. Published for the first time!

The Compleat Ova Hamlet — Parodies of SF authors by Richard A. Lupoff – A brand new edition with more stories and more illustrations by Trina Robbins.

The Secret Adventures of Sherlock Holmes — Three Sherlockian pastiches by the Brooklyn author/publisher, Gary Lovisi.

The Universal Holmes — Richard A. Lupoff's 2007 collection of five Holmesian pastiches and a recipe for giant rat stew.

Four Joel Townsley Rogers Novels — By the author of *The Red Right Hand*: *Once In a Red Moon*, *Lady With the Dice*, *The Stopped Clock*, *Never Leave My Bed*

Two Joel Townsley Rogers Story Collections — Night of Horror and Killing Time

Twenty Norman Berrow Novels — *The Bishop's Sword*, *Ghost House*, *Don't Go Out After Dark*, *Claws of the Cougar*, *The Smokers of Hashish*, *The Secret Dancer*, *Don't Jump Mr. Boland!*, *The Footprints of Satan*, *Fingers for Ransom*, *The Three Tiers of Fantasy*, *The Spaniard's Thumb*, *The Eleventh Plague*, *Words Have Wings*, *One Thrilling Night*, *The Lady's in Danger*, *It Howls at Night*, *The Terror in the Fog*, *Oil Under the Window*, *Murder in the Melody*, *The Singing Room*

The N. R. De Mexico Novels — Robert Bragg presents *Marijuana Girl*, *Madman on a Drum*, *Private Chauffeur* in one volume.

Four Chelsea Quinn Yarbro Novels featuring Charlie Moon — *Ogilvie, Tallant and Moon*, *Music When the Sweet Voice Dies*, *Poisonous Fruit* and *Dead Mice*

Five Walter S. Masterman Mysteries — *The Green Toad*, *The Flying Beast*, *The Yellow Mistletoe*, *The Wrong Verdict* and *The Perjured Alibi*. Fantastic impossible plots.

Two Hake Talbot Novels — *Rim of the Pit*, *The Hangman's Handyman*. Classic locked room mysteries.

Two Alexander Laing Novels — *The Motives of Nicholas Holtz* and *Dr. Scarlett*, stories of medical mayhem and intrigue from the 30s.

Four David Hume Novels — *Corpses Never Argue, Cemetery First Stop, Make Way for the Mourners, Eternity Here I Come*, and more to come.

Three Wade Wright Novels — *Echo of Fear, Death At Nostalgia Street* and *It Leads to Murder*, with more to come!

Eight Rupert Penny Novels — *Policeman's Holiday, Policeman's Evidence, Lucky Policeman, Policeman in Armour, Sealed Room Murder, Sweet Poison, The Talkative Policeman, She had to Have Gas* and *Cut and Run* (by Martin Tanner.)

Five Jack Mann Novels — Strange murder in the English countryside. *Gees' First Case, Nightmare Farm, Grey Shapes, The Ninth Life, The Glass Too Many.*

Seven Max Afford Novels — *Owl of Darkness, Death's Mannikins, Blood on His Hands, The Dead Are Blind, The Sheep and the Wolves, Sinners in Paradise* and *Two Locked Room Mysteries and a Ripping Yarn* by one of Australia's finest novelists.

Five Joseph Shallit Novels — *The Case of the Billion Dollar Body, Lady Don't Die on My Doorstep, Kiss the Killer, Yell Bloody Murder, Take Your Last Look.* One of America's best 50's authors.

Two Crimson Clown Novels — By Johnston McCulley, author of the Zorro novels, *The Crimson Clown* and *The Crimson Clown Again.*

The Best of 10-Story Book — edited by Chris Mikul, over 35 stories from the literary magazine Harry Stephen Keeler edited.

A Young Man's Heart — A forgotten early classic by Cornell Woolrich

The Anthony Boucher Chronicles — edited by Francis M. Nevins
Book reviews by Anthony Boucher written for the *San Francisco Chronicle, 1942 – 1947.* Essential and fascinating reading.

Muddled Mind: Complete Works of Ed Wood, Jr. — David Hayes and Hayden Davis deconstruct the life and works of a mad genius.

Gadsby — A lipogram (a novel without the letter E). Ernest Vincent Wright's last work, published in 1939 right before his death.

My First Time: The One Experience You Never Forget — Michael Birchwood — 64 true first-person narratives of how they lost it.

A Roland Daniel Double: The Signal and The Return of Wu Fang — Classic thrillers from the 30s

Murder in Shawnee — Two novels of the Alleghenies by John Douglas: *Shawnee Alley Fire* and *Haunts.*

Deep Space and other Stories — A collection of SF gems by Richard A. Lupoff

Blood Moon — The first of the Robert Payne series by Ed Gorman

The Time Armada — Fox B. Holden's 1953 SF gem.

Black River Falls — Suspense from the master, Ed Gorman

Sideslip — 1968 SF masterpiece by Ted White and Dave Van Arnam

The Triune Man — Mindscrambling science fiction from Richard A. Lupoff

Detective Duff Unravels It — Episodic mysteries by Harvey O'Higgins

Automaton — Brilliant treatise on robotics: 1928-style! By H. Stafford Hatfield

The Incredible Adventures of Rowland Hern — Rousing 1928 impossible crimes by Nicholas Olde.

Slammer Days — Two full-length prison memoirs: *Men into Beasts* (1952) by George Sylvester Viereck and *Home Away From Home* (1962) by Jack Woodford

Murder in Black and White — 1931 classic tennis whodunit by Evelyn Elder

Killer's Caress — Cary Moran's 1936 hardboiled thriller

The Golden Dagger — 1951 Scotland Yard yarn by E. R. Punshon

A Smell of Smoke — 1951 English countryside thriller by Miles Burton

Ruled By Radio — 1925 futuristic novel by Robert L. Hadfield & Frank E. Farncombe

Murder in Silk — A 1937 Yellow Peril novel of the silk trade by Ralph Trevor

The Case of the Withered Hand — 1936 potboiler by John G. Brandon

Finger-prints Never Lie — A 1939 classic detective novel by John G. Brandon

Inclination to Murder — 1966 thriller by New Zealand's Harriet Hunter

Invaders from the Dark — Classic werewolf tale from Greye La Spina

Fatal Accident — Murder by automobile, a 1936 mystery by Cecil M. Wills

The Devil Drives — A prison and lost treasure novel by Virgil Markham

Dr. Odin — Douglas Newton's 1933 potboiler comes back to life.

The Chinese Jar Mystery — Murder in the manor by John Stephen Strange, 1934

The Julius Caesar Murder Case — A classic 1935 re-telling of the assassination by Wallace Irwin that's much more fun than the Shakespeare version

West Texas War and Other Western Stories — by Gary Lovisi

The Contested Earth and Other SF Stories — A never-before published space opera and seven short stories by Jim Harmon.

Tales of the Macabre and Ordinary — Modern twisted horror by Chris Mikul, author of the *Bizarrism* series.

The Gold Star Line — Seaboard adventure from L.T. Reade and Robert Eustace.

The Werewolf vs the Vampire Woman — Hard to believe ultraviolence by either Arthur M. Scarm or Arthur M. Scram.

Black Hogan Strikes Again — Australia's Peter Renwick pens a tale of the outback.

Don Diablo: Book of a Lost Film — Two-volume treatment of a western by Paul Landres, with diagrams. Intro by Francis M. Nevins.

The Charlie Chaplin Murder Mystery — Movie hijinks by Wes D. Gehring

The Koky Comics — A collection of all of the 1978-1981 Sunday and daily comic strips by Richard O'Brien and Mort Gerberg, in two volumes.

Suzy — Another collection of comic strips from Richard O'Brien and Bob Vojtko

Dime Novels: Ramble House's 10-Cent Books — *Knife in the Dark* by Robert Leslie Bellem, *Hot Lead* and *Song of Death* by Ed Earl Repp, *A Hashish House in New York* by H.H. Kane, and five more.

Blood in a Snap — The *Finnegan's Wake* of the 21st century, by Jim Weiler

Stakeout on Millennium Drive — Award-winning Indianapolis Noir — Ian Woollen.

Dope Tales #1 — Two dope-riddled classics; *Dope Runners* by Gerald Grantham and *Death Takes the Joystick* by Phillip Condé.

Dope Tales #2 — Two more narco-classics; *The Invisible Hand* by Rex Dark and *The Smokers of Hashish* by Norman Berrow.

Dope Tales #3 — Two enchanting novels of opium by the master, Sax Rohmer. *Dope* and *The Yellow Claw*.

Tenebrae — Ernest G. Henham's 1898 horror tale brought back.

The Singular Problem of the Stygian House-Boat — Two classic tales by John Kendrick Bangs about the denizens of Hades.

Tiresias — Psychotic modern horror novel by Jonathan M. Sweet.

The One After Snelling — Kickass modern noir from Richard O'Brien.

The Sign of the Scorpion — 1935 Edmund Snell tale of oriental evil.

The House of the Vampire — 1907 poetic thriller by George S. Viereck.

An Angel in the Street — Modern hardboiled noir by Peter Genovese.

The Devil's Mistress — Scottish gothic tale by J. W. Brodie-Innes.

The Lord of Terror — 1925 mystery with master-criminal, Fantômas.

The Lady of the Terraces — 1925 adventure by E. Charles Vivian.

My Deadly Angel — 1955 Cold War drama by John Chelton

Prose Bowl — Futuristic satire — Bill Pronzini & Barry N. Malzberg .

Satan's Den Exposed — True crime in Truth or Consequences New Mexico — Award-winning journalism by the *Desert Journal*.

The Amorous Intrigues & Adventures of Aaron Burr — by Anonymous — Hot historical action.

I Stole $16,000,000 — A true story by cracksman Herbert E. Wilson.

The Black Dark Murders — Vintage 50s college murder yarn by Milt Ozaki, writing as Robert O. Saber.

Sex Slave — Potboiler of lust in the days of Cleopatra — Dion Leclerq.

You'll Die Laughing — Bruce Elliott's 1945 novel of murder at a practical joker's English countryside manor.

The Private Journal & Diary of John H. Surratt — The memoirs of the man who conspired to assassinate President Lincoln.

Dead Man Talks Too Much — Hollywood boozer by Weed Dickenson

Red Light — History of legal prostitution in Shreveport Louisiana by Eric Brock. Includes wonderful photos of the houses and the ladies.

A Snark Selection — Lewis Carroll's *The Hunting of the Snark* with two Snarkian chapters by Harry Stephen Keeler — Illustrated by Gavin L. O'Keefe.

Ripped from the Headlines! — The Jack the Ripper story as told in the newspaper articles in the *New York* and *London Times*.

Geronimo — S. M. Barrett's 1905 autobiography of a noble American.

The White Peril in the Far East — Sidney Lewis Gulick's 1905 indictment of the West and assurance that Japan would never attack the U.S.

The Compleat Calhoon — All of Fender Tucker's works: Includes *Totah Six-Pack*, *Weed, Women and Song* and *Tales from the Tower*, plus a CD of all of his songs.

Totah Six-Pack — Just Fender Tucker's six tales about Farmington in one sleek volume.

RAMBLE HOUSE
Fender Tucker, Prop.
www.ramblehouse.com   fender@ramblehouse.com
228-826-1783   10329 Sheephead Drive, Vancleave MS 39565

LaVergne, TN USA
18 August 2010
193855LV00001B/11/P